Hellsong Series

Infidels: Cris

SOULFALL

SHAUN O. McCOY

SISYPHEAN PUBLISHING

This is a work of fiction. The damnation portrayed in this novel is fictitious, and similarities between it and any actual damnation are strictly coincidental.

Soulfall

Editor-in-Chief: Gabrielle Olexa
Associate Editors: Matt Michaelis, Justin Williams, Leigh Thomas
Consulting Editors: Paris Ward, Amanda Simays

Title art: Thomas the Younger
Title Layout: Kirill Simin

A Sisyphean Publishing Book

Http://hellsongseries.com

ISBN-13: 978-0692504369 (Sisyphean Publishing)
ISBN-10: 0692504362

First Edition August 2015

Printed in the United States of America

0 9 8 7 6 5 4

PRAISE FOR SHAUN O. McCOY AND THE HELLSONG SERIES

"By the end of Soulfall my hands were shaking."
—*Monet Jones, Author of the Trace Trilogy*

"McCoy is a talented and bright young writer. Knight of Gehenna is a new kind of novel—a page turner in the truest sense—wrought from equal parts brawn and brain."
—*B. Butler, Author of Murder in Cairo*

"McCoy is a brilliant writer; insightful, intelligent, articulate, imaginative, and funny."
—*McKendree Long, Author of No Good Like it is*

"McCoy masterfully creates characters, scenarios and the Hell where they live. He writes with a passion, layering emotion on fantasy and science fiction, drawing in readers from beyond his genre."
—Ginny Padgett, President of SCWW

"Shaun is the real McCoy."
—*Laura Valtorte, Filmmaker, Author of Family Meal*

"McCoy again mixes freakishly paced action with deep emotion and a subtle plot. Soulfall blurs the lines between genres: one part Fantasy, one part Science Fiction, one part Literary Fiction—this sequel delivers."
—*Matt Michaelis, Author of Kids Summon*

"McCoy will certainly go to Hell for writing Soulfall . . . but it was probably worth it.
—*Justin Williams, Author of Blind Faith*

OTHER WORKS BY SHAUN O. McCOY

For Taylor
(May she find this on New Year's Eve!)

ACKNOWLEDGEMENTS

I'd love to take the time here to thank the Sipub team for working so hard to make this sequel a reality.

And of course, I need to thank you, the reader, for all the fanmail, reviews, and facebook messages.

SOULFALL

From Neostoicism: Philosophia

I have never wished to cater to the crowd—for what I know they do not approve, and what they approve I do not know.
—Epicurus

I'm not particularly disturbed by the fact that you, in a fit of self-deceit, devised a deity for yourself to worship. What bothers me is that the deity you created is a malevolent and bigoted fool. Truly, is this the best your imagination has on offer?
—Endymion

Q puts his hands on either side of my head. His calloused palms flatten the tears running down the sides of my face. His fingertips press into my hair. His thumbs push into my cheekbones. He pulls me forward until our foreheads touch.

"Listen to me, Cris," he says.

I won't listen. I don't want to listen.

I try to turn away, but he doesn't let me.

"I said *listen*."

For some reason, I nod my head. Jesus fucking Christ. I'm supposed to be a God damned infidel.

We don't cry.

"Look at me, Cris," Q orders.

Our heads are too close for me to focus on him, and my vision is filled with tears, so all I see is a blur.

"Are you listening?" he asks me.

I nod my head again.

"Your son is in a lot of pain. A lot. It's not the kind of pain that a person can stand. He screams whenever he's awake. I don't know if I've ever seen anyone hurting that badly."

"I know."

I can hear Aiden even now, whimpering in the next room. He's not conscious, but he moans in his sleep. He tosses and turns no matter how much of the ferment the infidels give him.

They said he was going to get better. I killed half of Hell to make damn sure he was going to get better. We brought him to El Cid so she could fix him. We did what we were supposed to do.

It wasn't *supposed* to be like this.

"We can't keep him like this," Q tells me, "even . . . even if we wanted to."

No shit. And of course we don't want to. We're going to help him. We're going to get Aiden fixed.

We are.

"I know," I say. "We've got to get him somewhere. To someone."

Q takes a deep breath. His hands drop from my face to my shoulders. I hadn't realized he'd been supporting me. I slouch under my own weight. Under my shot nerves. Under the sleep deprivation I'm suffering after tending to my son for two straight days.

Under my sorrow.

He exhales. "Cris, if you were . . . just imagine you were hurting that badly. Or that you were only conscious for an hour here, and a half hour there. Or that your sleep was filled with nightmares—"

"I know," I say quickly.

I don't have to imagine. I've been through that. On Earth, I died of cancer.

He steps back from me, but I still can't see shit.

His hands grip my shoulders more tightly. "If you were in that position, wouldn't you want someone . . . well, wouldn't you want to die?"

No.

Fuck no.

I hear my inner demons singing in my ears. Suddenly I'm standing straight. How could he? I shove him away. "The hell's wrong with you!" My heart explodes with anger. Blood rushes through my veins. I feel snot running out of my nose—snot and some blood.

Guess I'm not healed yet.

I push him again.

Fuck him. Fucking shithead. What the fuck does he think he's saying?

"Cris." His voice is maddeningly calm. "You may have to put him down."

Aiden's a human being. He's not some dog. He's not a horse. You don't put *people* down.

My head is spinning. "No."

Q steps close to me again. "He's in pain, Cris."

I shake my head. "You said the next Hell is worse. You said it hurt worse. You said we don't put people down."

"Cid's cut out his wight flesh half a dozen times,

but it regrows. He's not coming back from this."

"He will!" I hear my voice crack.

"He's hurting. He's in . . . in agony." Q is still calm.

"I don't fucking care!"

"We keep him asleep all day, but you've seen him writhing in his dreams. He's screaming himself hoarse. Cris, you need to let go."

"He's going to make it."

"You are torturing your own son."

I take in a deep, deep breath.

No. He's wrong. I'm not. Aiden can make it. They said he could. El Cid said it would be hard, but that he was going to make it.

He doesn't deserve to suffer. He doesn't. It's not *his* fault his mom was a devil-loving, kidnapping cunt. Aiden didn't know any better. He was just doing what his mother told him to. He didn't know wightdust would do this to him. He didn't know.

And he and Jenner had been getting along. They were even playing together. He'll get there, to that thing Cid talks about. Convalescence.

He'll reach convalescence.

I draw my pistol and point it at Q's head.

His eyes widen, then his hands rise slowly.

"Aiden doesn't die." The words barely come out of my mouth. I fight to keep myself straight, to suppress the sobs which threaten to double me over. "He doesn't die," I say more clearly.

"Okay. Okay." Q drops his hands, calm again. "It's your choice, Cris. You choose."

I feel a fire in my mind, burning like it did in Maylay Beighlay. If he dies, his mother wouldn't have won, not really. She wanted him to become a wight. And if it comes to it, that's what I'll do. I'll turn him all the way. I'll make him a monster that can go out and slaughter all the people I love. Anything to stop him from hurting, so long as he's alive. I won't kill my son. I won't. I won't let anyone do it, not even the Infidel himself.

Only turning my son *would* be killing him.

My gun is shaking.

"Cris, it's okay." Q says.

I bend over, nearly giving into the pain, and lay my pistol on the ground. Standing up seems like too much effort, so I don't.

Aiden is screaming again. Only his voice is so raw that the shouts break in and out.

Footsteps come from behind me.

I hear El Cid's soft, feminine voice. "Aiden will rest again soon." She wraps her arms around me and helps me up. "I've upped his dosage of the ferment," she says to Q. "His tolerance is getting higher. Has Cris come to peace?"

"He won't kill his son."

I feel one of Cid's small hands on my side. I look at her, her face also blurred by the tears in my eyes.

"I refuse," I tell her. "I won't let him die."

"Your opinion doesn't matter, Cris," she says with that infidel calm. "Your boy's does."

"But he doesn't understand! He only feels pain. He doesn't realize he'll get well."

The vague image that is El Cid's head shakes back and forth. "No. You do not understand. He's not getting well. It's his decision."

I reach down and grab my pistol again. I point it at her. Unlike Q, she doesn't seem to care. She turns her back on me and walks toward Aiden's room.

She's going to do it, she's going to kill my son.

I fire a warning shot at the archway over her head. The report echoes throughout the chamber. I hear the bullet ricochet off a far wall. The spent shell casing bounces and skitters across the stone floor.

Aiden's screaming becomes louder.

"The Devil help me," I say. "I won't let you kill him."

She keeps walking.

"I won't let you!"

I chase after her into my son's room, grabbing El Cid around her waist. She doesn't resist me and goes limp in my arms. I can see my son over her shoulder, lying on a stone slab. He's pale, paler than a corpse, as pale as a wight. His eyes are closed so tightly that his young face is lined with wrinkles. His back arches, a wave of pain washing over him. His mouth opens in a silent scream. Spit flies from his lips. For a moment his voice catches through his hoarseness, and I hear again his cry of agony. I can't watch this. I can't. Mercifully, the tears I'm holding back take away my vision.

I vaguely notice El Cid as she releases herself from my numb arms.

Aiden is breathing quickly. He sounds like he's hyperventilating. I wipe my eyes and force myself to look. His jaw is clenched against the pain.

El Cid kneels by his side, taking up his hand.

"Aiden," she whispers. "Can you hear me?"

He nods.

He mouths a pair of words.

"What, sweetheart?" El Cid asks him.

"It hurts."

"I know sweetheart," she says. "I know it does. I gave you some ferment a few minutes ago. You'll be asleep soon."

His nods come in jerks. His entire body is shaking.

"I want to ask you a question," she says. "A serious question. Can you focus long enough to answer it?"

He nods again.

"Just stay calm, okay? We want to put you to sleep this time in a way where you won't wake up in pain again. Would you like that?"

His nods come more fiercely.

"I'm not sure you understand, Aiden. You need to know we're going to kill you, okay? So that you don't feel this pain anymore."

His convulsions grow in intensity.

El Cid softly puts her hand on Aiden's forehead. "Do you want that?" She brushes his blond hair away from his eyes with her fingers. A few unruly strands fall back. "Do you want to die, Aiden?"

He tries to speak. His lips move, but barely a whisper comes out.

"I'm sorry, Aiden," El Cid says. "I couldn't hear you."

His fists clench at his sides, his back arches again. "I said . . . I said . . ." He bites his lip for a moment as the pain takes him. "I said . . . I'd have to ask . . . my father's permission."

Chapter 2

We huddle up, we six infidels, squatting down in a circle outside of Aiden's room. The low stone ceiling hovers just above us, bearing down on us like the weight of fate. Two squat black-marble pillars are in the room. One stands straight, formed in Corinthian style. The other becomes warped about halfway up, twisting and melding into the stone-brick wall as if it had been painted by Salvador Dali.

"The boy has chosen to live," El Cid says, her brow furrowed, "or at the least, deferred responsibility to his father." She motions toward me. "I know of no way to cure him. We need to find help."

One of the infidels is named Jessica. As best I can tell, she fucks both Eagan and Mason, two of the others in this huddle. How any group can stay on good terms while a woman is having her cake and eating it too escapes me, but now's not the time to question it.

Jessica leans forward into the huddle. "One of the ravens would be best. Muninn probably."

I have no idea what she's talking about, but I can

tell from Cid's frown that the idea won't fly.

"Too far," she says. "Muninn's probably deep in the Core right now. The boy's developing a tolerance to the ferment. We just don't have the time."

Mason screws his mouth to one side. "Now iffin' you worried 'bout supply, I got another batch, a whole canteen brewin'."

I remind myself that this man is not stupid. That drawl, and the fact that he likes to think things over slowly, might bring a person to that conclusion—but they'd be dead wrong.

El Cid is shaking her head. "Kid's only eight. An increased dosage is going to kill him."

"That's how it works in the old world," I say. "They kill cancer patients with painkillers, staying ahead of the pain."

Mason snorts. "Well thankya, son, for bringin' the bright light o' optimism to this otherwise morbid conversation."

At first I want to smack him, but for some reason I chuckle.

I guess my mood isn't so bad. Happens for some reason, after you cry. This, this I can bear. Us sitting here in this little hellstone chamber, discussing ways to save Aiden. It's terrible, but at least we're doing something.

"How much time do we have?" Jessica asks.

El Cid crosses her arms under her tiny breasts and

shrugs. "Impossible to know. A few weeks. Then we'll have to start backing off the ferment. His cries are bound to draw devils at that point."

Mason nods. "Might be they've drawn some to us now." He looks toward the arched stone entrance to our chamber, his hand dropping to the pistol holstered Eastwood style at his side. "And it's gettin' harder and harder to keep Keith and his boys at bay. They've got that durned wight helpin' 'em."

The Infidel Friend weren't the only outfit in Hell, I'd found. Keith was an enemy of El Cid, old baggage. That is, unless that wight working with him was Durgan. It's entirely possible he'd taken the death of the Archdevil personally and is coming after me.

Perhaps.

That'd be my baggage.

"A few weeks isn't enough time," Jessica says. "We could try to reach Endymion."

I wasn't really sure who Endymion was either, but at least I'd heard of him. He's a famous infidel. Q likes him, and Q is the best judge of character I know. Hell, Q didn't like Myla *before* she fell for that Archdevil.

"What do you think, Q?" I ask.

"Not enough time," he says. "Endymion is closer, but he's always on the move. Would probably take longer to find him than Muninn."

Q's face is as stoic as any infidel's, if not more so, but I've known him for a long time. A damn long time.

He's noodling some kind of plan.

El Cid picks up on it and zeroes in on him. The rest of the infidels follow suit, and we stare at Q together.

"What's your suggestion?" El Cid asks.

He raises both of his hands, his light brown palms held out to us as if in apology. "Nebuchadnezzar."

El Cid stands up. "Fuck."

"He works with undead," Q says. "He may not know as much about Hell as Muninn or Endymion, or even Ares, but he'll know all there is to know about half-turned wights."

Ares, there was a name I knew. I'd met him when I first came to Hell, when I was looking for Myla in the City of Blood and Stone. He's the one who introduced me to Q.

El Cid covers her mouth. She doesn't like the idea, but she hasn't ruled it out.

Jesus Christ, Q wants to take my son to a necromancer.

"I'd rather gamble on Endymion," Jessica says. "Hell, it'd be safer to root out Ares."

"Iffin' my memory any good, Nebuchadnezzar lives by the Pole. We get there mighty fast by my reckonin'. Beside, headin' to that beau will keep us clear of Keith and his wight."

Eagan is shaking his head, but he doesn't say anything.

I look to Cid.

She meets my gaze. "No, Cris. I won't do this. It's not worth risking my people. If more than one person dies trying to save your son, we will have made the wrong decision."

"Nebuchadnezzar isn't an infidel?" I ask.

Q shakes his head. "He knows *the* Infidel, but he's not one of us."

"The Pole is close, Cid," Jessica says.

El Cid puts her hands on her hips. "I'm aware that it's an optimal solution for saving Aiden, but I won't risk my people."

I stand up, too. "Fine, I'll go alone. Just like I did in Maylay Beighlay."

Everyone stands up now, except for Mason.

El Cid steps toward me. "Yeah? You fuckin' know how to get there?"

"I can find the Pole," I say. "I've been near there before. It's not so far from Maylay Beighlay, and I know which vein to follow."

"No," Q says. "Swinging by Maylay Beighlay would take too much time."

The frown lines on Cid's forehead disappear. "Okay. Cris, you and I will go. I won't risk anyone else."

"You're going to have to," Q says. "I'm going."

I love that man.

El Cid's green eyes narrow. "You are *not*."

Q smiles. "You going to have Cris carry Aiden the

whole way? Boy weighs almost as much as you. You feel comfortable carrying Cris' pack too? And taking point?"

"I do," she answers, "and he will. You're staying. That's an order."

Q bares his white teeth for a second. "I choose how I live, and how I die. Not you, not anyone else."

El Cid turns to her group. "Well the rest of you fuckers are staying out of this, or I'm taking us to Endymion."

"Ain't got to tell me twice," Mason says. "'Sides, give us a chance to kill Keith."

Eagan and Jessica nod.

I feel weak all of a sudden. My hands are shaking. I didn't understand half of what they said, but the important parts I have down. This Nebuchadnezzar guy is a necromancer, and because of that, he should know how to heal my son. So we're going to go to him and make him cure Aiden.

That's it, then. Me, Q and El Cid are going to save my boy.

Cid walks back into Aiden's room. I can hear her shuffling with her pack, getting ready to leave.

"Aiden lives," Q says.

I look at my best friend—my only friend. "Damn right."

Chapter 3

Jessica had fashioned me some damn nice shoes—damn nice. Their soles, made of hardened hound hide, were not much different than the hiking boots I wore in the old world, and the cut of their tread gave me a similar amount of traction. The dyitzu leather she used is dark, the red color of the devil dyed away. She even fastened some small metal rings to the holes through which the silk laces were threaded. I really can't fault her for anything about the footwear's quality—only that they were fucking miserable in the snow.

That snow crunches under my steps. Flakes of it melt, soaking through my socks and assaulting my feet with a toe-aching cold. I find myself hoping my feet go numb, but sadly, the hike is keeping just enough blood flowing to prevent that from happening.

I look out across the frozen icescape they call the Pole. It seems for all the world like an arctic wasteland. I cannot see the end of the chamber, but I can make out the ceiling. It's at least a mile high, and it gets even higher toward the center.

There was a trio of natives who'd followed us for a while after we entered, but I can't see them now. Maybe they've lost interest in us, or maybe they've fallen behind. It's hard to tell because they're wearing some kind of white fur that camouflages them against the snow.

Not us. Infidel black is stylish, but it makes us stand out like a neon shoot-me-please sign against the white background.

"Cris, you listening to me?" Q is asking.

Jesus Christ, how many times had he said my name before I noticed?

"Huh?"

"Your turn for Aiden."

Shit. Well, he'll take my mind away from my feet.

I let my backpack fall off my shoulders. It lands with a crunch, digging a few inches into the snow. I decide that I hate snow. Cid helps me unstrap Aiden's harness from Q, and then they fasten my boy to my back. I feel her tucking the blanket we use to keep Aiden warm around his body. His head rests on my shoulder. He stirs a little and his eyes open for a second. That's not a good sign. The ferment must be wearing off again.

El Cid pats me twice on my free shoulder to let me know we're ready to travel.

In the distance, miles behind us, tiny black dots move along a snow-covered hilltop. The natives? No, they'd be dressed in white. Someone else, then.

I point. "You see them?"

Q walks up next to me and scans the horizon. "Shit."

El Cid had already started walking onward, but she turns around at his curse. "What?"

"It's Keith," Q's low voice rumbles.

"Bullshit," I say squinting. "You can tell?"

Q grunts. "That's him."

Jesus.

I watch those distant specks disappear back behind the hill. "How the hell did they find us?"

"They must have a hound with them," Cid says. "I thought Jessica was going to hold them back, but I guess not. We better keep a hard pace. I don't think we have to worry much about them catching up with us in the short term. If we spend too much time with Nebuchadnezzar, though, we'll need to worry."

My lips are chapped all to hell. It actually hurts to talk because of it. "Much farther?" I ask.

"Twice as far as we've come," El Cid says.

Fuck me.

El Cid smiles, truly undaunted by our freezing surroundings. "Gives us plenty of time to get a better lead on Keith's men."

I feel Aiden's soft, even breathing on my neck.

"Nebuchadnezzar's magic had better fucking work," I say.

"First, he's as likely to try and kill us as help us," El Cid answers. "And secondly, there's no such thing as magic."

"You can call it whatever the hell you want," I tell her, "if a dead body gets up and starts walking around, I call it magic."

Q snorts, but El Cid seems genuinely curious in that little Socratic way of hers.

"Why's that?" she asks.

"Because . . ." I start with a normal tone of voice, but when Aiden shifts on my back, I continue with a whisper. ". . . because it ain't natural. Dead bodies don't just get up and walk around."

El Cid smiles as she takes the lead. Her braided black ponytail whips around her head as she looks back to me. "They don't. Takes corpsedust to make them move."

She must be dense. Maybe this infidel philosophy isn't all it's cracked up to be. "I don't see how dust is going to make a dead body start moving."

"Argument from ignorance," Q says.

I shake my head. "Your mom's ignorant."

Q grins.

"I tell you what," El Cid says. "If Nebuchadnezzar doesn't kill you and raise you in his thrall, you can ask him."

Q stops for a second, so we stop with him. Even with the weight of Aiden on my back, I march in place.

It's the only way to keep my toes from hurting.

Q focuses on El Cid.

"What?" she asks. "We've got to hurry now."

Q cocks his head to one side. "Only a moment. Are you going to be okay?"

I've seen exactly two emotions ever cross Q's face. Stoic, and more stoic. He's at more stoic now, which means he's probably torn about something.

El Cid's green eyes narrow. "Doesn't bother me."

"Why?" I ask Q. "Why would she not be okay?"

"She lost family in the Holocaust, Cris."

Holocaust, why the fuck would that matter . . . oh shit. "Who the hell are you taking me to?"

El Cid starts marching again.

Reluctantly, I follow. "Who?" I demand.

El Cid turns around, walking backward for a few steps. "He's a necromancer, Cris. You knew we weren't taking you to a choir boy."

Chapter 4

El Cid told me that Nebuchadnezzar, unlike any decent necromancer, hadn't waited to get to Hell before he began practicing his craft. He'd started early, inflicting horrific medical experiments on captured Jews. They didn't know about genes back then, at least not like we do now. Apparently the Nazis didn't believe in Darwin's natural selection. They believed in some Lamarckian epigenetic bullshit. Nebuchadnezzar was part of a project where they tried to change the eye, skin, and hair color of their victims in hopes of forcibly joining them and their descendents with the master race.

Maybe in this guy's mind it was better to do that than kill them.

Maybe.

Miles of snow pass beneath our determined and freezing feet, and during this march, I see no sign of Keith or his men. They're behind us though, I feel them on the back of my neck.

It ain't hard to pick out Nebuchadnezzar's compound. It might be two stories, or two and a half, and it's set into the side of the Pole chamber's wall. The fact that he built the thing out of ice bricks makes the structure look a bit like a castle—and I shit you not—there's a God damned ice swastika carved into a three foot circular depression over the arched entranceway. There's a woodstone door there, too, except the wood is darker and redder than most woodstone I've seen. He might have gotten the lumber from hungerleaf trees, except—I look around this icy wasteland—I have no idea where he'd have gotten it.

Q wanted to go in hot, guns out and ready—or barring that, sneak in. He even suggested we climb up the side of the Pole's wall and descend down into the compound. We think alike, Q and I. We want to negotiate from a position of strength.

El Cid countermanded him though. Said we'd "estrange" Nebuchadnezzar. Said he wouldn't want to help us. Besides, with Keith behind us, we may not have time to pull that off.

I guess I'm kind of happy she's in charge on account of how fucking impossible it was going to be to climb that ice cliff with Aiden on my back.

"Go ahead, Q," El Cid said, miming a knock in the air with one fist.

Q's white eyes widen incredulously under his raised eyebrows. "You want me to knock?"

El Cid smiles.

Q rolls his eyes and shakes his head. We approach the front door. Aiden whimpers a little. I put my hand on my pistol. Q looks me and Cid in the eye, one after the other, his hand raised and balled up into a fist. Then he turns back to the door.

He knocks four times.

And then four times more.

We wait.

Aiden's shivering pretty badly. It's making me shake. My toes are starting to go numb. I march in place a little, crunching the snow under the wonderful-but-completely-fucking-useless-in-snow shoes Jessica'd made me.

"Can we check—"

El Cid interrupts me by raising one hand, palm open. She cocks her head to the side and listens. For a second, all I hear is Aiden's breath and the cold-ass motherfucking wind as it blows across the Pole's ice and cuts through my clothes, chilling my bones—but then I hear it.

Step, step, drag . . . step. Step, step, drag . . . step. Step, step, drag . . . step. Q leans to one side, trying to look through the ice around the door. It's just barely transparent, and I see a figure approaching us. Step, step, drag . . . step. The ice bends the light pretty badly, so I can barely make out that it's a person coming. Step, step, drag . . . step.

I hear some sort of mechanism go off to the tune of grinding stone. Another dark shape, maybe the size of a boulder, lowers on the far side of the almost opaque wall. As it does so, the door opens. Inch by inch, a corpse is revealed.

Its pale face is long and almost devoid of rot. Perhaps the ice helps keep it fresh, I don't know. It's dressed in dark clothes that are very similar to an old world suit. It only has a black undershirt beneath its tattered blazer, and wears a pair of worn yet fashionable back dress shoes. Grey, literally lifeless eyes stare at us from within their sunken sockets.

It does not bare its teeth or mutter gutturally. It does not raise its arms or begin to charge toward us.

Instead, it bows.

We follow the dead thing through the halls of this ungodly ice castle. Step, step, drag . . . step. There are no decorations, just ice. The floor, thankfully, is rock, so walking isn't all that difficult. It's still cold in here, damn cold, but the fact that the wind isn't blowing makes things a little more tolerable. None of us have any real winter weather gear. Step, step, drag . . . step. I start to wonder if we can get hypothermia or something. Probably wouldn't be wise to spend the night in the Pole.

Undead Jeeves here is an odd thing indeed, but not outside the realm of my experience. In Maylay Beighlay, the old man who saved me before he died had also not attacked me. He'd brought me food each day while he was alive, and did so one last time after his death.

The corpse leads us down a tunnel which dead ends into yet another ice wall.

"A secret passage?" Q asks as we make our way down the hallway.

Step, step, drag . . . step. Jeeves keeps his left leg in the lead at all times. He makes two stutter steps, drags his back leg even with his front, and then finally moves his left foot forward. Even as far as corpses go, this guy isn't winning any races.

Aiden moans, a little louder than I'd like.

"He needs ferment," I say.

El Cid nods. "Shortly."

At least his shivering has lessened. My thighs are burning from the effort of walking with him strapped to my back.

Step, step, drag . . . step.

Undead Jeeves walks straight up to the wall. Step, step . . . then he pauses. He shuffles around and bows at us.

"I don't understand," Q says. "Is there an opening in the wall?"

"We're idiots." El Cid snorts. "We just followed a fucking corpse."

Q rolls his eyes.

"There were some stairs back there," El Cid says.

"Let's see if Nebuchadnezzar is on the second floor."

Jeeves bows again.

Now that the corpse is close to us, I notice some very odd scarring around its head. It's almost like a headband, curving around his temples and rising over the dome of his skull.

"What's up with this?" I ask, pointing to the dark grey scar.

El Cid leads us back down the hallway. "From a leucotomy."

This time, the corpse is following us.

I'd never heard of that. "A what?"

"A lobotomy," Q clarifies.

El Cid nods. "You perform it on a living person. If you do it right and treat the surgical incisions in the brain with rustrock, then when you raise the poor bastard as a corpse, they're usually not violent."

I look back over my shoulder at Jeeves. He bows.

"Sorry, buddy," I apologize to him.

El Cid takes us up a single flight of ice stairs. She moves lightly, with perfect balance. Q follows with similar grace.

It doesn't work that way for me. I slip on the first stair and have to catch myself, hands flung outward as I fall forward. Aiden whines. The cold in my palms is excruciating. I look behind me and see Jeeves bow again.

"Fuck you too, buddy."

I struggle to my feet. I lean up against the ice wall to my right for balance, head bowed forward under Aiden's weight, and try the next step. And then the next. And then the next.

El Cid and Q wait for me at the top of the staircase.

I hate this shit.

I'm breathing hard by the time I get to the top of the small flight. The fog of my breath settles on my nose as condensation.

I hate the Pole.

Oddly, the ceiling on the second floor is higher, and more work has been done on the decor. Rather than non-descript ice-brick hallways, many of the walls here are made out of single sheets of ice. Dead bodies are suspended in some of them, arrayed in unsettlingly artistic ways. They stand in grotesque mockeries of famous sculptures. Here, an Aphrodite with the arms missing. There, a Diomedes with genitalia properly worn away. I spot a corpse in the pose of the Thinker. The Thinker is a nude, white man. His face distorted from the ice as I walk toward him.

His chin rests neatly on his upraised fist.

Nebuchadnezzar is fucked up in the head.

The Thinker's eyes open and I almost lose my balance on the icy floor.

Nebuchadnezzar is good-and-real fucked up in the head.

The Thinker is a corpse—a damn well preserved one. If it wasn't for his eyes being blue, I'd think he was a wight.

"Over here," Q says, leaning up against an ice sheet wall which doubles as a window.

We can see the Pole through it.

He motions at a distant hilltop. All I see is a white wasteland.

"They're building an igloo," El Cid says.

Q nods.

I still can't see it.

"You think they're settling down for the night?" Q asks.

Finally I spot them, tiny black dots huddled around a white dome.

El Cid says, "Probably, but hard to know. Keith has proved wily so far. Let's not underestimate him."

I hear someone walking up the steps. My hand drops to my pistol again and I turn. Jeeves looks at me, and he bows. Then he turns around and walks back down the stairs.

Jesus.

"These bodies are corpses," Q says, pointing toward the suspended Thinker.

"Yeah, no shit, asshole," I whisper.

El Cid makes a chopping motion, her hand passing in front of her face. That's her cut-it-out-right-fucking-now gesticulation. In deference to her, I shut the hell up.

Step. Step. Step.

Is that Jeeves on the stairs? No, I can hear him, too, in the room below.

Step, step, drag . . . step.

But they're getting softer, the other footsteps are getting louder.

Step. Step. Step.

These are bootsteps, at times crunching the ice crystals on the floor. I see the grey blur of a man walking on the other side of the far wall.

Step. Step. Step.

His image becomes crystal clear as his figure passes by one of the ice sheets. He's got black boots, maybe made out of rubber. Their tops are hidden under an all grey overcoat.

Step. Step. Step.

He stops in a doorway and looks at us.

I have never seen a man more Aryan. His hair is very blond, though it is just dark enough to where I wouldn't call him a towhead. Even from across the room, I can tell his eyes are blue—a light blue, made to look almost grey by his overcoat. Two lightning bolts, made out of silver, adorn his collar. Not just lightning bolts, I realize. That marking signifies the SS. Well one thing's for sure, this man hasn't let the past go.

"Grüße Ungläubigen," he says, whatever the fuck that means.

"Guten Tag, Schweineficker," El Cid says.

I can only hope she just called him a pig fucker.

"Come," Nebuchadnezzar answers, unperturbed by whatever the hell she just said. "I've started a fire for you. Best not to waste it."

Fire? I wiggle my toes in my frozen shoes.

Hell, maybe he's not all bad.

Aiden moans in his sleep as we follow the necromancer through the ice halls to his parlor room.

"It's okay, son," I whisper. "Soon it'll all be okay."

It strikes me now that Nebuchadnezzar deals in death. As far as he's concerned, he might like my son better as a wight.

Nebuchadnezzar's parlor room is exquisitely designed. He's got a table made of the same dark red wood as the outside door. The fireplace is a half dome of ice set into the wall. Fire burning under ice — it makes no sense to me. Maybe it's a Hell thing, or maybe it's something that just works. I remember that Eskimos used to light fires in their igloos.

Either way, the fire burns peacefully in its icy fireplace beneath its icy mantel. A stack of dry logs, the Devil knew where they'd come from, lies on one side. On the mantelpiece is a golden eagle, its proud head in profile. For a second I think it's American, then Roman, then I realize it must be a Nazi relic.

"We need to administer medicine to the boy," Cid tells Nebuchadnezzar. "He might resist."

The Aryan necromancer waves a gloved hand toward the empty table. "Be my guest."

He has no accent, not a German one at least—and there is something quaint about his voice, something that reminds me of old movies. Black and white ones, maybe, or the ones that came out just after where the color wasn't quite right. It's a decidedly *American* accent. Not British at all.

Oh hell, now I understand. I add spy to his list of negative attributes. Nazi war criminal, necromancer, and spy.

Q unbuckles Aiden from my back. I help unwrap my boy's blanket and lay him down on the table.

Aiden gives a shout.

"It'll be fine, young one," El Cid whispers to him. "Drink this, the pain will go away."

He struggles anyway, closing his mouth and turning his head. Sometimes it's like this. Sometimes he fights us.

"Hold him down," El Cid orders.

Q grabs one arm and puts his other hand on Aiden's shoulder. I do the same. Aiden twists his head back and forth, shouting. El Cid jumps up on the table and sits on his chest, putting one leg out past me and over his shoulder. She reaches with one hand and cups the back of his neck. She leans away, pulling his head up.

"His mouth, Cris."

I work at his jaw. "It's okay, son. Drink this, it's okay."

He opens his mouth voluntarily, which is a relief, but even so, I can't watch his pain anymore. I look to Nebuchadnezzar instead. There's no expression on his face, and that bothers me. At first I can't tell why. After all, I'm surrounded by infidels, and none of them are particularly expressive. But this guy's face really is expressionless—not stoic. He honestly doesn't care. The whimpering calls of my dying son, the cries which tear my heart asunder, which shake the universe of my mind, which cause my fists to clench and my blood to boil and my soul to die—they don't mean a damn thing to Nebuchadnezzar.

"Cris," El Cid says.

"Huh?"

She touches my arm. "You can let go now."

Aiden has stopped struggling. Q has already backed away. My son is still in pain, but he's fighting it well. There's a strap El Cid has been letting him bite down on. He's biting the hell out of it now.

El Cid hops off the table, somehow landing on the ice floor as if it were stone. Nebuchadnezzar and Q are moving gracefully, too, but I'm sliding every few steps. It's got to be Jessica's damn boots.

"My apologies," El Cid says.

Nebuchadnezzar shrugs. "You have not come for a social reason, I assume. That boy, he's on edge, isn't he?"

El Cid looks at Aiden's shaking form. "Yes."

There are eight chairs around the table. He walks to the one at the head, closest to the fire, and pulls it back. Each chair has been made out of what looks like wicker. Maybe from dried sinfruit vines or something . . . but again, I have no idea where he'd find that around here.

Nebuchadnezzar flashes a set of white teeth at us and motions to the fire. "You have until the fire burns out, then you must leave."

His voice bugs the shit out of me. It sounds like the voice of a hero. Like that of a clean-cut man. I could shove coals down his throat and fix that.

Later. I can do that later.

El Cid and Q sit down on the left side of the table while I take a seat on the right. I scoot my chair closer to Aiden, reaching out with two fingers to touch his cool, clammy forehead. El Cid raises her hand, palm open. She doesn't make that chopping motion, but I can tell she wants to. I get the hint. She wants to do this negotiation, so I shut my mouth.

El Cid's green eyes narrow. "We've come to ask you for help with the boy."

Nebuchadnezzar smiles. "I'd heard you infidels are the keepers of knowledge."

"We try. We don't have time to make it to those of us who know enough."

His smile widens and those white teeth glint in the

firelight. "I can't imagine you'd think *I'd* be willing to help you."

El Cid comes slowly to her feet. "I don't know why you think you have the right to live," she whispers, her chair toppling behind her. "Maybe you could take this moment as one of absolution? Maybe you could use all that perverse knowledge you've gathered to heal someone?"

Her words don't faze him. There's something about Nebuchadnezzar's smile that unsettles me, but what? Ah, it's that the smile is real. It touches his eyes. He's genuinely happy at her suffering. At mine, at Aiden's. That, or he's so good at acting as to be completely unreadable. Either possibility makes him pretty damn monstrous.

"Such anger," Nebuchadnezzar notes. "Did I take someone from you? Did my people?"

El Cid shrugs. "You did, right before my people took away your Reich."

I'm all for her. Fuck him, you know. But damn, Cid, Aiden needs his help.

Q leans forward. "Even if you won't help, studying him should be something that is . . . edifying."

Nebuchadnezzar stands. He loosens each finger on the glove of his right hand before he pulls it off. "Strip the boy, I'll take a look."

He tosses the glove on the table.

I notice Jeeves entering the room.

I bow to him, and he bows back.

Q and I strip Aiden. He looks so small. Skin and bone, his little muscles long and stringy on his arms and legs. His blue veins stick out in the cold—and they turn black at the dead portions of his body. Goosebumps rise from the living flesh, but don't where he's turned wight. He's not all the way unconscious yet, and he covers himself with his hands.

Nebuchadnezzar opens one of Aiden's eyelids and peers into the dim eye. "You've cut out the dead parts to see how they grow back?"

"Yes," El Cid confirms, "they come back as wightflesh."

"His soul is on edge." Nebuchadnezzar's hands move across Aiden's chest. "How long has he been like this?"

"A week," El Cid says.

The man's blond eyebrows arch up with a detached curiosity. "I'm amazed the stilling hasn't taken him. He's got a very strong will."

El Cid says, "Stubborn fucktardedness runs in the family."

Jeeves bends down and picks up the chair El Cid had knocked over. I bow to him. He bows back.

Nebuchadnezzar purses his lips. "I owe the Infidel nothing. You understand? *Nothing*. I have no reason to help you. I have many experiments going on right now, and I don't have time to try to help you. Kill him now, or, when his will does break and the stilling takes him, that part of his soul which is wight will spread like cancer. When he rises, he will just be that much harder to put down."

It's my turn to speak. "Is the life of a wight worth living?"

The room goes silent except for the crackle of the fire and the step, step, drag . . . step of Jeeves.

Nebuchadnezzar's blue eyes focus on me intensely. "Are you even an infidel?"

"He will be soon enough." There's an odd glint to El Cid's eyes, like she's proud of me or something.

"So you owe the Infidel nothing," I say quickly, "but what if I owed you something. I can get things for you, or kill someone for you. You name it, I don't care what."

"Cris!" Q warns me. "You cannot put your soul into the hands of this man."

That warm-seeming smile touches the necromancer's eyes again. "You must be the stubborn fucktard."

I nod.

Nebuchadnezzar looks to the dismal fire. "Your time is almost up."

I pull my shirt over my head and toss it into the fire. "Please. I'll watch your experiments. I'll run them if I have to. Is there *anything* you can do to help my boy? Anything? Did you ever have a son?"

Those blue eyes go cold.

I had done it. I'd touched a nerve. It had been a shot in the dark, but I'd just nicked whatever was left of the soul of that monster.

The fire flares up, consuming my shirt in a blaze.

He picks up his glove from the table. "You, your Jew, and your nigger have nothing I want."

It's Q's turn to show his infidel colors, and he does so beautifully. I'm almost unsure if he even heard the slur.

I stand, sliding the chair back. I catch it before it tips over and smile apologetically toward Jeeves. He bows.

"Then I'll get you something you want. Anything. I'll go anywhere."

Nebuchadnezzar sneers at Aiden. "You don't have time. I saw how much ferment you gave him, and I know you infidels make it strong. You've got a week, maybe a week and a half at most. You're useless to me."

"We can teach you things," I blurt out. "How to make infidel fire. How to—"

He gives his German laugh. "The Infidel himself already came and taught me about necromancy. You know nothing I need to know."

"Then we'll kill you!" I shout.

Nebuchadnezzar shakes his head. "I don't care."

"Then I'll kill your undead. The ice statues. I'll kill Jeeves." I stop.

Nebuchadnezzar seems confused. He doesn't know who Jeeves is, of course.

"You mistake me for someone else, infidel-to-be. I have no friends."

Suddenly I know what he wants. Suddenly I know what I can give to help him.

"Eva," I say.

Nebuchadnezzar's head jerks up. Twice, twice I've touched his nerves.

"You heard me," I say. "Eva Braun. I know where she is—was, rather. I know where she appeared in Hell. You'd be able to track her."

He takes a half step forward.

"She was looking for her sister's husband," I continue. "Some SS guy, so she might have left."

He looks away. "I'm not a member of the Party anymore."

Suddenly I feel the cold on my bare arms and chest. "I don't think she is, either."

The fire is almost out.

"I'd have nothing to say to her." Nebuchadnezzar's mask is almost back on.

"No?" I ask. "Isn't there anything you'd like to ask her?"

Those baby blue, master-race eyes are in turmoil.

I look to El Cid. I know what she is thinking. She's thinking that I'm lying. I know I'm not supposed to lie, but Hell, I'm only an infidel in training. And it isn't completely a lie. I had heard the rumor.

He turns to Jeeves. "Hansel, get this man a shirt. Shirt? You understand. Shirt."

Jeeves bows and walks away.

Step, step, drag . . . step. Step, step, drag . . . step.

"Very well, I will help, you stubborn fucktard," Nebuchadnezzar says.

"That's Cris for short," I tell him, my heart leaping in my chest. "No 'h,' to avoid confusion."

I turn to Q. He's grinning.

Aiden lives.

Chapter 5

It's seriously cold as fuck in here. I blow into my hands to try and warm them, but my breath just isn't enough. If anything, the moisture that collects on my fingers makes them colder.

"So you do know a way to help save him?" El Cid asks.

I haven't known El Cid very long, but the bitch has an ego on her. I think this is going to piss her off. She won't like having to admit someone can think of something she can't.

"I do," Nebuchadnezzar says, "but the solution is something I can't say while the lad is present . . . asleep or no. These are words even his unconscious should not hear."

Q picks my boy up off the table and rests him over one shoulder. With his free hand, he grabs a wicker chair. "We'll be in the other room."

There isn't a man in Hell like Q. I can't even say how much he's done for me—but I can't let him do this.

"I need your opinion, Q," I tell him. "Set Aiden

down outside. He'll be safe enough." I turn to Nebuchadnezzar. "Won't he?"

His Aryan head nods.

Step, step, drag . . . step. Step, step, drag . . . step. Jeeves, or Hansel as Nebuchadnezzar calls him, has returned, a shirt in his hands.

El Cid's eyes narrow.

She's not happy to see this. I'm not sure how hard it is to make an undead follow your commands, but I wouldn't have thought it possible. Maybe Jeeves is just a leper that's *really* far gone.

Step, step, drag . . . step. He bows to Nebuchadnezzar and offers him the shirt. The Nazi shakes his head and points at me. Jeeves turns, handing me the shirt.

El Cid takes in a quick breath.

It's a black, soft thing, thick. I put it on quickly.

"You can make them talk, too," Nebuchadnezzar says to Cid. "Did you know that? The Infidel taught me how."

El Cid's green eyes bore into him.

He gives that genuine-ass smile again. "You mean to say he fucked you, and never told you about these things?" Suddenly his German accent comes through a little. "He did fuck you, didn't he? That's what they say, you know. The Infidel and I talked about many things when he came here. Maybe one of them was your cunt, do you think?"

She crosses her arms beneath her small breasts. "Look here, Planck dick, how long is this cure going to take?"

The necromancer's face becomes serious. He pauses for a second as Q joins us.

"Once you're on edge," Nebuchadnezzar says, "you almost always end up being a wight. Think of the soul as something that tries to heal itself. If there's just a little bit of wight corruption, the living side will heal it out. Only, the wight part of your soul is trying to heal itself too. That balance, I've induced it in people. It's a damn painful thing. Never seen anyone last for more than a day."

Aiden has been on edge for a week. But then again, I'm not sure Nebuchadnezzar's subjects had much to motivate them.

I wonder what it is that keeps my son alive. Love? Hate?

"But it is curable?" Q asks.

"It is," Nebuchadnezzar answers. "In fact, even if you become a wight completely, it's still curable—only you need their cooperation."

El Cid's tiny jaw opens a little. "You're shitting me."

"No shitting," he says. "Understandably, for practical reasons, that cooperation is impossible to get. But with your boy, we may be able to manage it."

"I'm listening," El Cid says.

"This Hell, like Earth before it, is *objective*. If your son were to die, and go to the next Hell, the Hell you infidels call Sheol, he could believe himself into health because it's *subjective*. Now obviously, coaching your son how to heal himself in Sheol now and then killing him to send him there would defeat the purpose . . . but there is a place where Sheol and Gehenna meet."

I have no fucking clue what they're talking about. "You want to say that in English, buddy?"

El Cid ignores me. "The Erebus. You want to take him to the Erebus."

Nebuchadnezzar nods. "Now the mind can play tricks on a person, particularly a boy. It's best if we don't leave it up to his will. We'll tell him that the Erebus will cure him if he stands in it, that way his expectation will—"

"It won't work," El Cid interrupts.

Nebuchadnezzar crosses his arms and sits down again at the head of the table, leaning back into his wicker chair. He kicks up his black boots onto the table, flinging particulates of ice across the dark wood. "Do tell."

"The subjective changes don't stick," she says. "He'd have to stay by the Erebus for the rest of his life."

That's not good news, but it is better than nothing. "I'd rather that than see him die."

"There are Furies at the Erebus, Cris," Q says. "The rest of his life at that point would be about ten minutes."

Nebuchadnezzar is smiling. It's the creepiest motherfucking smile I've ever seen, but right now, I'm hoping like hell he knows something we don't. "The Infidel usually uses a statue as an example for the subjective nature of Sheol being temporary, does he not?"

"You take the statue to the Erebus," El Cid says in agreement. "You change it with your mind. When taken back, it will slowly revert to its original state."

Nebuchadnezzar's grin splits his face.

"Tell us," Q snaps.

"I'll wait for you to figure it out."

I really fucking hate this guy. Fortunately, El Cid's smart as fuck.

"Slowly," she says.

"Correct," Nebuchadnezzar answers. "Aiden won't be on edge. If we take him away from the river slowly, only parts of his soul will revert into being a wight."

Q starts nodding, too.

"Will someone please explain this to me?" I beg.

"It's like a wound," Q says. "If I took all your skin, you'd die. But if I took away the same amount, little by little over a series of weeks, you'd heal. Sheol will *pretend* restore your son, but as we move back, if we move back slowly enough, your son's healing will be real. Eventually, as the pretend falls away, all that will be left is Aiden."

El Cid's brow furrows. "We need to get there quickly. The fastest route would be through the Carrion, but I won't risk it."

"Why not?" I ask.

She doesn't bother answering the question, but she doesn't need to. I'd traveled with Myla through the Carrion briefly on our way out of the City of Blood and Stone, and the place had defined the word hellhole.

Nebuchadnezzar gets up and moves to the fireplace. He puts a log on the coals of the fire and stands back. "Wouldn't work anyway."

"You know what," I say, "I've about had enough of this shit. Just tell me what we need to fucking do."

El Cid ignores me again. "Why not?"

"Imagination doesn't become a sense until you're nearly in Sheol," Nebuchadnezzar says. "Just marching up to the edge of the Erebus probably wouldn't do it. If he can't feel his own soul, he won't be able to heal it — or, not enough, I believe. You've got to get him practically across the river before his mind will even be able to touch what it's supposed to believe into health."

El Cid leans forward, her lips curling into a smile. "Soulfall."

Nebuchadnezzar nods.

Soulfall. That sounds familiar. I've heard that before, when Q was telling me about the Infidel.

"We can take the Pole's tributary to the river

Janus," Nebuchadnezzar says. "Switch up to the Northern Lethe at Maylay Beighlay."

El Cid puts a hand to her chin. "Can't. It's gone dark."

"Maylay Beighlay?" Nebuchadnezzar asks.

El Cid frowns. "We can switch over at Dendra."

"I hate that place," Q says. "They'll confiscate all our weapons."

El Cid shrugs. "They'll give them back when we leave."

Soulfall. It had something to do with the Infidel and Lilith. Something to do with—

"We can even stop at Portsmouth on the way," Nebuchadnezzar says. "If we're lucky, we could get there in two weeks. Can you keep the boy alive that long?"

"I can sure as hell try," El Cid answers. "We can ease up on the ferment at times, but the boy's cries might bring enemies to us."

"Best to ease up now," Q says. "It'll be much more wild near the Erebus."

"And the Furies?" El Cid asks.

Nebuchadnezzar breathes in deeply as he looks up in contemplation. "I can distract them. There are undead on top of Soulfall. I can make them harmless. That little touch I give them will make them targets of the Furies. It will buy us some time. Not much time, but perhaps enough."

Soulfall. Now I remember.

It's where the Infidel committed suicide so that he, like some mad Orpheus, could chase his lover into Sheol and try to rescue her. Where the currents of the Erebus river tore a city away from Hell to leave it hanging between this damnation and the next. Where the survivors of that calamity were driven insane by the awful power of Sheol.

Where I'm headed.

But none of that matters. Like always, I didn't understand everything the infidels said, but I don't need to. The important bit is that we have to take my son to Soulfall. What matters is that Nebuchadnezzar can get us passed whatever those Fury things are. What matters is that once we get there, Aiden will live.

Chapter 6

The ice cave is lovely, bright, and deep. It snakes around from the back of Nebuchadnezzar's keep and curls into the edge of the Pole's wall. Ice stalagmites and stalactites rise and fall to meet each other like the broken-tooth maw of an angry hellhound.

My balance isn't getting any better, but at places the ice floor gives way to loose rock, and Jessica's boots finally find some traction.

Behind us, moving with surprising grace, is a wight larger than I would have thought possible. It's unsettling enough that this necromancer could control wights in the same way that Minotaurs and Archdevils can, but worse than that, this person couldn't have died at his current size. Nebuchadnezzar had to have done something to create this eight foot muscle-bound monstrosity besides tattooing that ridiculous swastika on its forehead.

Balanced over one of its comically broad shoulders is our boat, a red, wooden gondola, long enough to hold the five of us. I'm not sure who made the damn thing, but it looks like it had been plucked straight from the set of some Venetian movie—with one major difference. Its prow is high and shaped in the form of a curve-necked Chinese style dragon.

"You're not afraid to leave your experiments behind?" I ask Nebuchadnezzar.

He shakes his head.

"Why'd you cage up Jeeves, or Hansel? Whatever his name is."

Nebuchadnezzar's blue eyes squint at me. "It's necessary to cage him."

"Why, though?"

"Otherwise he'll take over."

I chuckle a little—not because this Nazi fucker is funny—but because I need his ass to save Aiden.

"You know why I help you?" He asks me.

I look back to make sure Aiden is asleep. "Yeah, because all you Nazi fuckers have a hard-on for Eva."

He shakes his blond head. "No. Well, perhaps. But I saw the way you interacted with Hansel."

"Oh?"

"A man who can empathize with a corpse might be open minded enough to see me fairly."

Wait until he finds out what my "open mind" thinks of him.

There's a drop where a section of the floor, now a smooth ice sheet, forms a steep ten foot decline. El Cid and Q hop down, sliding on the soles of their boots with their inhuman balance. Fuck. Why can't I do that shit?

I stop at the dip and put my belly to the floor, feet facing down, keeping Aiden away from the ice. The cold hurts my fingers. I slide. To my horror, the giant wight-thing glides down, boat and all, like the infidels did. Nothing that big should move so smoothly.

Nebuchadnezzar follows, scooting down on his ass.

Q looks confused and is paused at the mouth of two different ice caves. He points down one and looks to Nebuchadnezzar.

"That's it," the Necromancer says.

The path becomes more rocky, and the ice stalactites drip water into pools. Small rivulets of running water begin collecting in the center of the tunnel. The melting ice should mean that the cave is getting warmer. If it is, though, I can't feel it.

Nebuchadnezzar is looking at me as if he'd asked me something. Oh right, the shit about me being open minded.

"Why would you care if I judge you or not?" I ask.

He doesn't answer, but I realize how lonely it must be for him. Not that he doesn't deserve it.

"Look," I say, "I'm not trying to *see* you, or judge you. I'm a father who needs you."

His genuine-ass smile splits his face. "We shall see, Cris with no 'h.' We shall see. But your friendship is of little matter. You will take me to Eva."

"Yes, or to where she was."

He looks at me, as if considering that I might be lying to him for the first time. Wish thinking will trip anybody up, even a Nazi. Hell, considering they opened a second front against Russia, *especially* a Nazi.

I do my best to keep my face unreadable.

The caves must be getting even warmer as we keep moving because more of the ice is melting. I still can't feel it, though. There must be some sort of heat cycle in here, because otherwise wouldn't these caves have all melted away? Or at least, that seems right. Who knows? Hell is a strange beast.

Cid would know.

"You sure we need the golem?" She asks, motioning to the eight-foot wight. "If the boat is really that heavy, I don't know how we'd port it."

Nebuchadnezzar shrugs. "We could take him with us."

Q snorts. "You can *try* and take that thing through Dendra."

Nebuchadnezzar laughs. That German guffaw is getting on my nerves.

"The boat is light enough," he says. "And the Creature will stay."

The water is filling up the middle of the cave's floor. It's really starting to look like a stream now. I hear the rush of a larger river ahead, and the sound is comforting.

"How much farther?" I ask. "I might need to pass

Aiden on."

Nebuchadnezzar looks at my boy. "The Creature can carry your lad—but only a few more chambers, to answer your question."

I look at the wight. Hell no. I'd rather Aiden spend time with his mother than that thing.

El Cid freezes, her hand dropping to the pistol at her hip. "Nebuchadnezzar, are any of your undead in these caves?"

The necromancer shakes his head. "When I first cleared them out, there were a few Kharas Bolge, but no longer. Nothing can survive that cold water long enough to get this deep into the caves."

"I heard something," Cid warns.

"Your own fear, perhaps," Nebuchadnezzar says.

Maybe he's right, but Cid don't scare easy.

As Nebuchadnezzar said, the small river we're following joins a big one, perhaps twenty feet across. The ice ceiling hangs low enough that the boat on the monster's shoulders starts breaking away some of the icicles.

Some stranger starts shouting from a crevasse across the river. "No! They're not! The infidels are on *his* side."

El Cid and Q dive behind some human-sized ice stalagmites.

I look toward the yelling, seeing three men dressed in white. Their guns are leveled at us.

Shit!

I reach around behind me and clutch at Aiden's harness, keeping him close. I backpedal madly, turning my body toward the guns to shield him from any incoming bullets.

Nebuchadnezzar is about as fast as me.

"Creature—" he begins.

A shotgun blast rings out and a sudden spray of pulverized ice erupts from the stalagmite by my head, shards scattering across the floor. Two rifle reports follow, hitting the Creature.

"—back!" Nebuchadnezzar yells.

Together, the necromancer and I take cover in the passage that leads to this chamber.

I reach for the buckle at my waist.

The Creature seems unharmed by the bullets. It obeys its master, and comes back, boat and all, rushing toward us. I duck below the gondola as it passes by.

"Help me!" I shout to Nebuchadnezzar, pointing a thumb behind my back to Aiden.

"How might I assist?" The necromancer is as calm as ever.

"Hold him up!"

Another shotgun blast sends ice crystals flying into our chamber. Some of them end up in my eyes.

I blink them away. "Jesus!"

I kneel down and work at the buckle. My freezing fingers are stiff and unwieldy. I feel Aiden's weight lifting off of me, so I know Nebuchadnezzar has my son. Fucker will probably try and use him as a shield.

"If he dies, you die!" I shout as I get the buckle undone.

I slide out of the harness and draw the Old Lady. She's a Smith & Wesson Model 916A pump action 12 gauge shotgun with a 28 inch barrel.

The walls of the tunnel are ice, so I try and see through them to my enemies. No luck. I look around for something to toss—something to draw their fire so I can get a shot off. Nothing.

I'll have to wait for Q and El Cid to return fire.

But they don't look like they're trying to fire back, they're huddled down behind their stalagmites.

The hell?

I rip the blanket off of Aiden and throw it out into the open. Two rifles and a shotgun fire. I turn the corner in an instant, the Old Lady ready.

"No!" El Cid yells.

I jerk back quickly, slipping on the ice and landing on my ass safely back in the passageway.

"What the hell, Cid?" I struggle back to my feet. "They're shooting at us."

"They're here to kill Nebuchadnezzar, Cris!"

"No shit! And we need him."

"He's evil. Under different circumstances, *we'd* kill him. We can't shoot these people for being good!"

You've got to be kidding me. The infidels are

famous for their pragmatism, their willingness and ability to win over the loss of their loved ones, but I'm beginning to think that I could give them a few lessons.

"This ain't the time for moral judgments!" I shout.

To help my argument, the strangers fire another round of buckshot.

"See?" I yell over a rifle shot. "They're not interested in our neutrality. So help me God, Cid, if they cross that river I'm gunning them down."

Even from this distance I can see Cid's frustration. "You will not! Neb's got to fight this one on his own."

Neb shrugs. "The Creature will dispose of them."

Well that's good.

Fuck. That's not good. Those people are going to die. Or worse, Nebuchadnezzar is going to die.

The idea gives me pause. Do we really need him? We already know where to go. The idea of betraying the guy now makes my stomach a little queasy—but I can handle that.

No. We do need him for something. The Furies. He's going to distract the Furies. Damn it.

I peek out into the cave. One of them is slinking behind some rocks by the river. Shit, I think he's found a crossing. If he gets to our side, he'll have an angle from which he can shoot right at me.

Another shotgun blast showers me with ice crystals. A light mist hangs in the air where the buckshot hit, slowly dissipating.

I've had enough.

"Hold your fire!" I shout. "I'm coming out."

"We'll kill you!" one answers.

It strikes me as odd that he'd warn me about that, like he doesn't actually want to shoot me.

"I'm coming out!" I repeat.

"Any friend of Nebuchadnezzar deserves to die."

He's got a point. "I hate that fucking bastard." I turn to the necromancer and speak softly

to him. "Sorry to throw you under the bus."

He shrugs the shoulders of his grey overcoat. "Throw away."

He's set Aiden against the cave wall. My boy's kicking in his sleep, probably because the gunshots are disturbing his ferment coma.

I throw my Old Lady out into the chamber.

"Before you go," Nebuchadnezzar says, "tell me where to find Eva, in case you die."

Prick.

I shake my head and storm out into the chamber, my hands held high. "Please don't fucking shoot!" I shout, my voice shaky. "I just want to talk, okay?"

I'm not dead yet, so I take that as a good sign. I slip a little. I need to be careful. Another jerky motion might get me killed. I pick my way across the icy rocks. The rush of the river is a gentle thing. A peaceful thing. I try to let it soothe my nerves, but my adrenaline is racing.

I see them more clearly as I get closer. One is still

behind cover, his rifle trained on me. The other two have stood up from behind their rocks. They're both bearded. One looks Mexican, the other white. They're clad in what looks like layered dyitzu fur, only it's snow colored. Maybe they found some way to bleach it. All three of their guns, two rifles and a shotgun, are all leveled at me.

I make my way slowly down the uneven trough which ends with the stream.

I stop at the bank. "Please, let me explain this to you."

The first stranger tosses down his rifle and comes out. "No, let *me* explain this!" He charges down to his side of the river, his breath misting in the air. "When Keith came and warned us about you, we thought you'd come to kill Nebuchadnezzar. I thought I could trust infidels. We figured Nebuchadnezzar would sneak out the back, so we came to help you, and look what we've found! You've decided to help *him?*" He points back to the cave where I left the necromancer. "Do you have any idea what he does? And to think I defended you infidels when Keith warned us."

Sooner or later, we've got to kill that Keith bastard. No time to think about that now.

I clear my throat. "I know he raises corpses but—"

"He's brought back my *daughter!*" The man's voice is shaky. "He keeps her there in his castle of ice. Keeps her as his *bride.*"

After a moment, I realize my jaw is open. I look back over my shoulder to the cave where Nebuchadnezzar is hiding.

Oh, he's going to die. I might do it right now.

"Cris!" El Cid shouts. "Do not do anything stupid."

"I'm just fucking full of stupid today," I shout. I turn back to the man. "You're a father, so you understand me. Your daughter's gone, but my son is still alive . . ."

He draws his pistol and points it at me. "I don't give a *fuck*."

"Q!" I yell, my voice sounding hoarse. "Get my son."

There's silence.

"Q, I told you to get my fucking son." I hear the last of my echo. Q's tall black figure stands up from behind his stalagmite.

The poor father across from me holsters his pistol. I watch Q walk with that infidel grace across the ice. He disappears into the passageway. For some reason I start tearing up when he emerges, my son limp in his arms. I hold the tears back.

Infidels don't cry.

"Come on," I offer the father. "Come on around. Let me show you why a good human being like Q will work with a man like Nebuchadnezzar."

He stands in indecision for a moment. I can tell that this man, only twenty feet or so away from me, is in turmoil. The steam of his breath fills the air and dies away. Fills the air and dies away. Finally, he nods.

He turns around, walks back up the bank, and scoops up his rifle.

Q and I wait with my unconscious son. The man wanders along the river a ways and jumps over the water where it narrows.

"You are very brave," Q tells me as we wait.

I shake my head. "I'm glad you approve."

"Don't be too glad," Q says. "I'll take it back if you get shot."

Aiden is so pale in his arms, as white as this cave. His blond hair is sticking up in the cold. I reach out and smooth it with my numb fingers.

"I'm going to kill Nebuchadnezzar when this is done," I mutter.

Q shakes his head. "You made a deal."

"With a corpsefucker."

"Indeed."

The father walks up to us, his rifle held across his chest. His eyes are on Aiden.

"Is he . . . a wight?"

I shake my head. "Halfway. On edge, they call it. And there is a chance we can save him, a small one, but a real one. We need Nebuchadnezzar to do it."

The man stares at Aiden. He looks to the ceiling and lets out a deep breath. The air fogs with his exhalation, billowing upward toward the stalactites above. He covers his eyes for a second. Then, with that hand, he reaches out and grabs me by the shoulder.

"You have no idea," he says through clenched teeth, "no idea how much I want to kill him."

I nod, and then check back over my shoulder toward Nebuchadnezzar. "Maybe not. But I'm starting to get an idea."

"I don't want your boy to die," he says. "Is there no other way?"

Q shakes his head. "Trust me, if there was, we wouldn't be working with a man like that. El Cid, back there, she ordered me *not* to do this. It's the love that Cris holds for his son that has made us compromise ourselves so."

The father takes another deep breath, sending more fog into the air.

"Well, he'll be out," I say. "You could raid his keep while we're gone. Save your daughter from undeath."

"Is he taking that monster wight with you?"

I grimace. "No."

He covers his face with his hands.

"If you fear you cannot beat the Creature," Q says, "then you should know that if we leave, Nebuchadnezzar will send it against you. It does not matter, logically, whether Nebuchadnezzar is with us or not."

Sometimes Q's straightforward thinking just doesn't help.

"This isn't a logic question, Q," I say. "Some things you fight for, win or lose. Children are one of them." Now I put my hand on the father's shoulder. "Which is stronger with you, your pain at losing your daughter, or your empathy for the hope I have of saving my son? You give the word, and I'll stay out of the way. But if you let me go, this much I promise you, I'll make sure Nebuchadnezzar makes it back here so you can have a chance to kill him."

He shakes off my hand and turns his back to me. He walks over to the river and kicks a chunk of ice into it. The current drags it swiftly along, knocking it against the bank a couple of times before I lose sight of it.

He turns back and looks at Aiden. Q shifts, adjusting my boy in his arms.

Another breath.

"Save your son, Infidel Friend," he says, and walks away.

"Thank you," I answer.

Chapter 7

I'm not sure how long I slept, but the awkward position I did it in—one side propped up against the gondola and my head bent all the way back—left me with a sore side and a neck so tight I can't turn it all the way to the right. That, and I have a monstrous headache.

At least it's not cold anymore.

Q stands in the back of the boat, his alert eyes darting from right to left. Even as he does so, he moves the pole in the water, guiding us with peripheral vision, I suppose, down the waterway.

The river itself now has a regular stone bank, worked over by Hell's architect into the shape of bricks. The rock above us is similar, forming vaulted ceilings of dark red and black stone. Sometimes that ceiling is so low that Q has to be careful not to hit it with his pole. I even see him duck under one arched overhang.

I work at my neck with my fingers, but they hurt like hell, too. Maybe I've got a bit of frostbite or something. Hell, I might have just slept on them.

El Cid is sleeping somewhat more gracefully than

I'd managed. Her knees are tucked up to her chest, her chin resting between them. Nebuchadnezzar and my son are in the front of the boat. Aiden is mercifully unconscious, and the necromancer seems to be sleeping as well.

"How long was I asleep?" I whisper to Q.

"Two hours," Q says, guiding us around a Doric pillar which rises out of the water, stopping just short of the ceiling. "Maybe three."

I yawn and try turning my head to the right again. No luck—pain shoots from my eyeball to my neck and then down to my ass. I redouble my massaging efforts, kneading deep into my shoulder muscles with my aching fingers before working my way up to my neck.

"And how long until Dendra?" I ask.

"Two days," Q says, "assuming we sleep in shifts."

I haven't had a good night's rest since Maylay Beighlay. I probably won't until after Aiden is cured.

"Devilsign?" I ask.

"Thankfully not," Q says. "Not yet. This river is far from tame, though. We'll face some dyitzu, no doubt, before you sleep again." He poles us gently forward. "I should warn you about Aiden."

Damn. "What?"

"As dangerous as this is, it's nothing compared to the Erebus. We'll be north of the Carrion, and that's good, but we'll need to be quiet. We've lessened your son's dosage of the ferment so that we can keep him sedated later. Besides, Neb over there says he needs to coach your boy, so . . ."

So, in the short term, he's going to be in pain.

"Okay," I say.

It's Aiden's voice that wakes me.

Somehow I'd managed to fall asleep in exactly the wrong position again. Jesus, and I thought I was sore before. I'm pretty sure I have a gondola shaped bruise starting on my buttocks and running up the left side of my body.

"But I like black," Aiden is saying.

This is as cogent as I've heard him in some time.

It's Nebuchadnezzar's accentless 1940s movie voice which responds. "But blue is the most beautiful color an eye can be. They used to give me lots of money to make sure that brown eyes could be turned to blue. You're lucky, to have been born this way. It shows you're an Übermensch."

Fuck. Well, I guess after spending time with his mother and an Archdevil, a little Nazi guidance can't do *too* much damage.

Aiden says something, but I can't quite make out his tiny voice.

"Don't say that," Nebuchadnezzar responds. "Your father loves you very much."

"Cris doesn't love me." Aiden's voice seems so terribly small, so terribly lost. "It's hurting."

"The powder I gave you will only last a little while longer, so you've got to concentrate while you can." Nebuchadnezzar says.

He gave my son what? I feel my blood heating up.

"I want to go back to sleep," Aiden says.

"You need to be strong," Neb replies, "for your father, like we discussed. We're taking you to a place which can heal you. You just have to concentrate on yourself. You won't be able to feel it here, but at the Erebus, when you let your mind wander, oh—the power you'll feel."

"Will it take away the pain?"

"Oh yes," the necromancer answers. "All your pain will melt off you. You'll feel strong, like you haven't felt in weeks. And you've grown up, boy. You might feel stronger than you ever have before. I need to teach you, to teach you how to heal yourself."

Aiden's next words seem forced. "I don't want to learn from you."

I sit up, startling Nebuchadnezzar. Waves of pain crash through my body, stemming from my ridiculously stiff neck.

"You do want to," I say.

"He's right," Nebuchadnezzar says.

Aiden shakes his head and his nostrils flare. "I don't have to get healed. If I get sick all the way, that'll end the pain too."

Nebuchadnezzar nods. "You're right, but you

won't be able to do either for some time. This thing I'm about to teach you, it will help with the pain. It will help you with the pain *now*."

"I don't need you!" Aiden shouts at the necromancer.

I shush him.

"It's not from me," Nebuchadnezzar says. "The most evil man I know taught me this."

Aiden's darkened eyes narrow in suspicion. "Then why did he teach you, if he was so evil."

Nebuchadnezzar smiles. "You'll have to learn to find out."

Chapter 8

El Cid's green eyes pop open. For a second I'm afraid she was awakened by the distant sound of some devil I could not hear, but she seems unworried. I feel along the side of my pack until I find the Old Lady. The grain of its smooth wooden stock makes me feel safer.

The river has grown wider and shallower. It might only be five feet deep in places, and in the lighter rooms I can see the smooth granite stone floor beneath it. The chambers still have those odd arched roofs, but they are broader now, and lower. Doric pillars stand in places, rising up out of the river, some reaching the ceiling while others stop short of it. As we move from room to room, we find pillars on the shoreline too, and at times they spring up all over like an odd sort of stone forest.

Nebuchadnezzar's voice, the one I think of as honest because it has a bit of a German accent, drones on in an even, hypnotic monotone that blends into the background white noises of the rush of the water and the gentle sound of Q's poling. "Worry not about each thought. Don't try not to think them, but categorize them as thoughts. Put them in a little bubble, recognize them, and move on. And if the pain distracts you, this is no worry. The pain itself is just another thought, in another bubble."

The exits to these rooms, all arches, are numerous and dark. For all I know, there's an army of devils waiting under those granite keystones. The idea causes the hair on the back of my neck to bristle.

"Now think of what you feel. Think of how you sense your entire body. The sensations, all of them, running up into your mind. Let's center your attention, for a moment, on your hand. Try, if you will, to lose any preconceived notion of its shape. Right now, you think you feel your five fingers, but this is an image which you have mapped onto the sensations. Try to feel, really feel, what your nerves are reporting."

I see scratch and burn marks along one of the pillars. There is some oily residue on the ceiling, too, as if a dyitzu's fireball had struck there and died out.

Devilsign.

I hear Q suck in air through his teeth as he sees it. El Cid sits up a little straighter.

The river leads us gently through another low arch and into a short tunnel before bringing us into the next room. It's broader than the last, with a thicker forest of pillars than we saw before. Some of the archways have a second level of entrances above, leading to even more tunnels—each as black as the eye of a wight.

Nebuchadnezzar's even voice does not stop. "It doesn't feel like five fingers, does it? Not if you really concentrate on what you feel. The sensations are almost like a nebulous cloud, about where your hand is. Focus on that. Now, when we're at the Erebus, you will feel that cloud connect with something, a mist in the air of a sort that you can't see, or smell, or touch. It's all around us, now, as we speak, but at the moment it is beyond your senses. When we're at the Erebus, you will *feel* it."

The next chamber is even taller. There's houndsign, too, I'm noticing. I see some of their burrows in a woodstone wall toward the back. It looks like the woodstone has healed a little, so I'm hoping these are the abandoned homes of hellhounds who left years ago.

"You will feel the mist even as you feel your hand," Nebuchadnezzar is saying. "But don't follow it outward, follow it inward. You'll see the mist is something that occupies the same space as yourself. As you move through it, you bring your soul with you. That soul now is made of two things. One killed by fire, the other by ice. When you get to the precipice, when you look out across that evil river, you'll feel the burning begin. It will race through your body and come up your spine with more power than even the pain you feel now. That burning will encompass you, but it will not consume you, and it won't seem quite like agony. It will seem like something else, like . . . convalescence."

I feel something—something in the air.

Anticipation? Fear? I can't quite describe it, but it's powerful. The bristling hairs on the back of my neck settle down because the waiting is over. I *know* what's coming. I glance at El Cid. Q's looking at her too. She nods.

"Nebuchadnezzar," Q says. "Come take the pole."

"I'm—"

"Now," Q's voice is calm.

I draw the Old Lady even as El Cid shoulders her M-16.

"Get Aiden down," she whispers.

It's their breathing, I realize. I can hear the breathing of devils, just barely, echoing throughout the chambers over the sound of the river.

Nebuchadnezzar's eyes grow wide and he moves quickly to the back.

"It's okay, Aiden," I whisper as I ease him down to the bottom of the gondola. "It's okay. We've got infidels on our side. We'll be fine."

The room erupts with fire.

Chapter 9

Fireballs stream in at us.

Our boat rocks as Nebuchadnezzar poles us to one side.

The dozen hunched dyitzu who threw them scatter behind their missiles, clawed feet clicking against the stone as their strangely humanesque strides carry them across the chamber. Their ruddy skin helps them blend in against the red and black background.

El Cid and Q's M-16s fire off three-round bursts in quick succession.

One dyitzu pivots, its clawed arm readied for another throw. It forms its fireball as I line up the Old Lady. The trusty shotgun booms and the buckshot catches the beast in the shoulder, sending it spinning to the ground. It starts to rise. I cock the shotgun, a spent shell whirling away, bouncing off the edge of the boat. My next blast is a slug. It blows the wounded dyitzu's head open, sending up a spray of blood, brains and bone.

The smells of gunpowder and hot copper fill the air

as the last trio of Cid's spent .223 shells tinkle along the wooden floor of the boat. One of the dyitzu is twitching, but none seem alive. Jesus, those Infidel Friend are efficient—but they've still got their guard up.

My ears ring in the sudden silence.

"There's more," Q warns.

"Many more," Cid clarifies.

Our gondola drifts over to the stone bank and collides with it. Our wake washes up against the rock, spilling water over the edges of the stones. Nebuchadnezzar begins poling us forward again, slowly, tentatively, his blue eyes darting left and right.

I load two more shells into the Old Lady.

There are perhaps two or three hundred shadow-filled archways set in two levels along the back of the room. I peer into those dark passages, fearing how many might contain dyitzu. I see one, its deep red humanoid torso just barely visible in a second story arch. Its legs and arms are hidden in the darkness.

"I see one," I report, raising the Old Lady to my shoulder.

"Hold," Cid orders.

The dyitzu I spotted was on the left, but Q is looking to our right.

"Is it clear?" Cid asks him.

"I don't know."

"I need to know, Q."

"I said I don't know."

"Then fucking guess!" she orders.

"Clear."

I see movement down a second archway. "Another," I say.

"The hell are they waiting for?" Cid asks as Q turns around and levels his M-16 to the left.

Nebuchadnezzar's poling keeps us away from the banks. I look down into the water as the granite riverbed passes below, but I don't see any devils lurking beneath the current.

We're about one hundred yards into the chamber, and we have about two hundred left to go. There's a small turn in the river near the end of the room that might prove to be difficult.

Jesus fucking Christ, this is weird. Dyitzu aren't known for their restraint. If something is organizing them, we could be in some serious shit. It's not like the river leaves us a whole lot of ways to avoid an ambush.

"The hell are they waiting for?" Cid asks again.

"I don't know." Q's voice is unsure.

"Hounds?" I ask.

Q nods. "I think I can smell them."

Fuck, smell them from the boat? Maybe. It's Q, so I give him the benefit of the doubt.

El Cid shakes her head. "Stop the boat, Neb."

The pole scrapes along the bottom, slowing us, but we're still moving.

"Push us to the side," Q orders.

Nebuchadnezzar follows Q's instructions. The boat, still drifting toward the center of the chamber, bumps against the granite bank with a thud. I reach out and put a hand on the slick stones to help hold us. Finally we stop.

"Out, Q," she orders. "Pull us back."

Q hops out of the gondola with his preternatural-infidel balance. He loops the strap of his M-16 around a corner of the back of the boat. With the help of Nebuchadnezzar's poling, Q pulls us slowly upstream.

Our progress against the current is terribly slow.

"You think they'll let us out of this room?" I ask.

Cid shrugs.

"Are we going to find another way around?" Nebuchadnezzar asks.

She shakes her head. "This is a feint."

And it's working. I hear the echoes of dyitzu claws clacking against the stone as they run, unseen in the darkness behind the arches. The sounds fill the chamber. There must be a hundred of them.

Aiden sits up, his face in agony.

"Down, son."

"I need ferment." Tears are in his eyes.

"Down!"

He does as he's told.

Q struggles on as the dyitzu claws continue their movement.

"Just a bit more," Cid says.

Q nods and keeps on pulling.

I see a dyitzu in an arch on the second level. It's leaning forward, eager, not even bothering to hide itself. This one's skin is a dark brown. I can see its bald head, and though the dyitzu is too far away for me to make out its black eyes, the devil turns slowly with our progress.

"Now!" Cid yells.

Her M-16 rings out as she looses a pair of three-round bursts. I see one dyitzu slump forward out of his arch as the boat switches direction. The boat rocks and Q jumps in.

"Pole!" He shouts. "Pole, Neb!"

The grey-coated necromancer, his face contorted with a grimace of fear, slams his pole down into the water. He works it frantically, pushing us faster and faster with the aid of the current.

The archways light up as the hidden dyitzu there form their fireballs. I see them, for a moment, standing behind their foot-wide infernos. They're bunched up in the arches near the upstream side of the chamber, a testament to their stupidity.

They'd fallen for Cid's trick.

"Defense, Cris!" Cid shouts.

The hell does she mean?

Her and Q open up, firing their three-round bursts.

I'm about to loose my own shot, but Nebuchadnezzar's sudden poling causes me to lose the bead on my target.

Again, the fireballs come streaking in at us.

Neb shoves the pole down, and we jerk as we slow suddenly. I almost fall onto my son but catch myself by posting my knee on the bench. The wave of fire rolls in ahead of us, exploding into showers of fiery raindrops as they burst on the granite bank or sizzling with steam as they bury themselves into the river.

One hits the front of our gondola, exploding into a shower of liquid fire. El Cid, standing at the prow, stops shooting as she steps over my son, straddling him and bending over.

The flaming droplets of the last fireball land on her. She spins around, her armored back still smoking as she takes aim again with her M-16.

While the first volley of fireballs came in a wave, the second is much more uneven. Nebuchadnezzar does his best to keep us out of the hellish rain, but it looks like a few are coming straight at us.

Ah, defense.

I loose two sets of buckshot at the incoming missiles. The spread tears up three of the fireballs as they come, sending their napalm-like conflagrations showering across the stones far short of our boat. As a bonus, some of my shot hits a dyitzu. A fourth fireball singes my shoulder as it rushes by, and I can feel its heat rake across my cheek.

We're about halfway, one hundred and fifty yards

to go.

I hear the growl of hellhounds.

They come, a pair of grey-coated dogs, five foot tall and four foot wide, tearing around the bend of the river.

"I've got them!" Nebuchadnezzar yells.

There is nothing to do but trust him.

I shoot down another couple of fireballs, but even so, one soars right past Cid's head. Bitch is so hard, she doesn't even flinch. She drops her clip into her belt and loads another with no wasted motion.

The dyitzu start pouring out of the archways, some dropping down from the second story.

The hounds are nearly on us.

I know Nebuchadnezzar says he's got 'em, but I can't help myself. I loose a shell in their direction.

I might as well have been shooting a BB gun.

Neb, one hand on the pole, produces a glass jar from his overcoat and tosses it. It shatters on the granite and the air fills with white dust.

My eyes start watering as we float through the chalky substance.

Oh Jesus, it stings. I feel it getting into the back of my throat.

"Loading!" I shout, my voice cracking from the burn of the dust.

But what it's doing to us is nothing compared to what it's doing to the hellhounds. They howl and screech and whine and bark. One is rolling around on its back, rubbing its face on the wet granite. The other is clawing at its snout so fiercely that it tears open wounds, the blood turning its grey fur red.

A pair of fireballs slam into the side of the boat, sending more liquid streamers of fire up into the air and onto the boat's floor. The flaming substance starts flowing toward Aiden.

I've only got two shells in, and a third slips from my fingers as I reach over and grab Aiden by the collar of his shirt. I jerk him up on the bench. El Cid is still firing.

The river pulls us out of the room.

The smell of smoldering wood fills my nostrils. I peer behind us through the smoke that's coming from our boat, the Old Lady raised.

There seems to be no pursuit.

El Cid pulls out some shells and starts filling up her clips. "Well?" she asks. "You gentlemen going to put out the boat?"

Chapter 10

Blood is dripping down from Aiden's mouth. Cid had given him his leather strap to bite down on after the fight, but only after he'd managed to chew a hole in his lip. Wight blood isn't a half-coagulated sludge like a corpse's. It isn't red like a human's either. It is a smooth, black liquid. Aiden's blood is something in between, like high-end motor oil.

It is inhuman.

A tree root has risen out of the water, snaking itself around a pillar before plunging up into the rock ceiling.

Wait, that doesn't make sense. The roots should go down, right? But the thing is thicker at the base than at the top, so I assume it's headed upward.

As the river and Q's careful poling takes us forward, I see more roots rising up from the ground and out of the river, constricting pillars into pieces or bending them like clay with their timeless grip.

My father, before he left me in the old world, used tree roots as a metaphor. Some roots had torn up the concrete in our driveway. He'd said some drivel about life being more powerful than rock. Well, maybe not drivel, maybe he was right.

"We're getting close," Q says, pointing at a particularly thick set of roots.

El Cid inclines her head in agreement.

I put my hand on Aiden's shoulder. He shakes it off. Beads of sweat are running down his forehead.

Q guides us around the dark mass of spiraling roots he'd pointed to. "You better medicate him now, Cid. If they suspect he's half wight, they won't let him in. We'll need to pass him off as a living boy."

"I can do it," Aiden says around the leather strap in his mouth.

"You're not looking so good," El Cid says.

He spits out the strap. "I *said* I can do it."

I love my son, so much. So God damned much.

El Cid turns and puts one of her tiny hands on my wrist. "Cris, if they find out he's on edge, they'll do more than keep him out of the city. They'll kill him."

"Try," I say.

Her eyes narrow in confusion.

"They'll *try* to kill him."

"Better clean that brackish blood off of his chin." Nebuchadnezzar is using his honest voice. "It's a dead giveaway."

El Cid hands me a little white handkerchief. Who knows where she gets all her damn knickknacks. My fingers brush over a pair of embroidered letters, a gold threaded "CW." The motor oil smudges on his skin when I attempt to clean it up. I dip the cloth into the water and try again.

There.

Much better.

I pass the handkerchief, un-cleaned, back to Cid.

"Thanks," her sarcastic voice replies.

Ahead of us, a series of those roots have climbed into a cavern, growing up along both sides of the fifty foot walls before spearing themselves in tangled knots through the stone ceiling. They create an overhang which creates a one hundred foot deep tunnel under which our gondola is about to go. A few tiny brown feathered white-breasted birds, which the infidels call psychopomp sparrows, nest amongst the flora. One flutters from one side to the other.

The longer I stay in Hell, the more terrible and beautiful it seems.

Two men, dressed in dyitzu skin and wicker hats, stand guard on either side of a small archway. Each is armed with a Winchester rifle. Q hops to the bank and brings the boat to a halt. I climb out and sit on the stone, my feet still in the gondola. I lift Aiden up and help him to the shore where he manages to stand on shaky legs.

"Infidels," one of the guards mentions. "Nebuchadnezzar, I never thought I'd see you associating with their kind."

Shit, I guess they aren't friendly.

Neb steps off the boat, his black boots squeaking loudly against the wet rock. "They're escorting me to Portsmouth."

It's as good a lie as any, I suppose.

The other guard frowns. "Better turn around then, Portsmouth has gone dark."

Fuck.

Nebuchadnezzar shrugs. "That's what they're here for." Neb jabs a thumb over his shoulder at us. "Don't worry, we've no plans to stay. We just need to switch our boat to the Northern Lethe."

The first guard glances back to his city. "We've got members of the Order in here, so you all are going to have to give up your weapons."

El Cid's hand instinctively goes to her M-16.

"Don't worry," he says, "we took their weapons too. We'll have the guns brought back to you. And be honest because we're going to pat you down."

The second guard speaks up. "There's an Infidel Friend in here already. Amirani. He's on good terms with the Tree Lord. I could have him escort you."

"That'd be very kind," El Cid answers.

The second guard disappears through the archway.

A drop of sweat runs down Aiden's brow. I can see him grinding his teeth.

"The boy okay?" the remaining guard asks.

"Yessir," I answer. "Took a bullet a ways back.

He's recovering, though."

Hell, Aiden's too pale for even that to make sense. A drop of his motor oil blood beads up on his lip.

I put my knuckle up to my own lip and meet his dark, dark eyes. He takes the hint and wipes his sleeve across his mouth.

I bend down, adjusting his clothes, and whisper, "Keep your head down, don't let them see your eyes."

He's shaking, from fear, perhaps, or from pain.

Hell.

He nods.

Q pats me on the shoulder.

With a series of heaves, he and I tug the gondola up onto the bank. For a boat, the thing is surprisingly light. Then comes the hard part. I have to divest myself of my weapons.

I drop the Old Lady, my 9mm, and my broken-pointed knife before them.

I never like giving up the .22 I keep at the small of my back, but hell, they did say they were going to give us a pat down. I add it to my pile.

"Your packs, too," the guard says.

Christ.

I toss my pack on my weapons.

The guard steps behind me. "Sorry about this, brother."

He begins his pat down by running his hands through my hair. Then he checks my under arms and all along my back.

"Drop your pants," he orders.

Jesus Christ, it's a damn thorough pat down.

Fucker even cups my balls before jamming a thumb up my asshole and running both hands down my pant legs.

"Shoes off," he says.

I roll my eyes, taking off the marvelous boots Jessica made me. He gives them a once over.

Q's next, and the guard is no gentler on him.

"El Cid," a voice calls from the archway.

I can tell the newcomer is an Infidel right away, and not just from the M-16 on his back. His bearing is too straight, his grooming too perfect, his—wait? How come he gets to keep a weapon? Four more brown dressed guards fan out around him.

Cid smirks. "Hi, Amirani."

Amirani motions to our stuff, and the guards start picking it up.

"I'm sorry, but this is necessary," he apologizes. "Just a warning, make sure you stick close to me when we get in. There was an attack on the grove last night, and the dyitzu are still occupying two of the trees. They've been throwing fireballs at us all morning."

Q is taking his boots off.

"Are you serious?" I ask, keeping an eye on Aiden. "There are devils in there and we can't even keep our guns?"

The guard picks up Q's boots, one by one, and shakes them.

Aiden is next. I feel my heart rate pick up.

Q and Cid don't even bat an eye. Nebuchadnezzar is similarly stone faced. I must be the only nervous one. Hopefully I'm keeping enough of my fear hidden to make them think I'm just an over-concerned parent—but I doubt I am.

"Dead serious," Amirani says to me. "The Order's got a cell visiting, and the Lord doesn't want any shooting. Normally we'd make an exception, but we can't this time."

"What's the Order?" I ask.

The man moves to my son, but he's got half an ear open to hear what Amirani is going to say. Here's to hoping he's distracted.

Aiden has his eyes closed. Smart boy. That little bead of dark blood is building up on his lip again and the wound itself doesn't look like a normal scab. I put my knuckle up to my mouth again as a signal, but with his eyes closed, Aiden can't see me.

Amirani says something, but in my worry I miss it.

"Well, Keith's one of them. They're a cancer, Cris," El Cid says. "They took some of our training, but they have shit for morals."

"They say the same thing about you," the guard remarks.

He begins running his hands through Aiden's hair.

Some of it comes out.

Oh, fuck.

"I bet they would," El Cid answers, "but the fact that there are no women in the Order should be a dead giveaway."

The guard shrugs. "Women soldiers aren't all that good."

"What are you doing so deep?" Amirani asks. "So far beyond . . . the Pale."

El Cid shrugs. "We're a little on . . . edge. This man," she motions to Neb, "he's got some business just past Porstmouth."

Amirani nods, his eyes two burning pits of infidel intellect. I suddenly get the feeling that he knows what's going on.

The first guard continues searching Aiden as the other four take our packs away.

"Wait!" the first guard calls.

The four stop, and so does my heart.

The man continues his pat down. "Come back for the boat."

Thank the fucking gods.

"Bullshit!" one answers. "We're not carrying that."

"Have to," the first guard shouts back. "Could be weapons in the boat." He turns to El Cid. "I'm going to have to cavity search you when I'm done with the boy."

Fucking perv.

Aiden flinches as the man cups his boyhood.

"Shoes," the guard demands.

Aiden, eyes lowered, takes off his boots. His toenails are black, and the dark blue veins in his feet make his extremities look like they were carved from marble rather than made of flesh. The guard's lips part as if he's going to say something.

Amirani speaks up. "If you want, Cid, I can do that part of the search. I'm sure the guard here won't object."

El Cid shrugs and shimmies her pants down to her knees. "I don't give a fuck." She looks at the guard. "Go ahead, shove your fingers on up there."

The guard absentmindedly shakes Aiden's boots as he stares at Cid's cunt. He drops them and begins to pat her down.

I let out a breath I hadn't known I'd been holding.

Aiden begins putting his boots back on.

I turn back to Cid. Her green eyes focus on me when the guard works his fingers into her. It is the most unsettling gaze I think I've ever received.

"Alright," the guard says, wiping his fingers on her pants. "You're clear."

El Cid pats the guard's ass as she walks by him. "It was great, thanks."

I put my hand around Aiden's shoulder and guide him through the archway.

"Sorry, Cid," I whisper.

She shrugs. "You'll make it up to me."

Chapter 11

In the twenty or so years I'd spent on Earth and the decade plus I'd spent in Hell, I ain't never seen a place like this.

The trees, more massive than even the giant redwoods I'd seen at Big Sir, grow *down*. There are perhaps two or three dozen of them, their massive roots—large enough to be trunks themselves—claw into the ceiling above while their branches spread, plunging into the bright mists below. Wooden walkways and wicker bridges line the limbs, sometimes spanning from tree to tree. Huts made of interwoven green matter nestle themselves into the nooks and crannies created wherever gnarled branches meet the irregular uber-oak trunks. A few of those psychopomps fly by us, swooping along the edge of the chamber before alighting onto a set of nearby branches.

Amirani leads us along a vine bridge which takes us from the chamber entrance to one of those wooden walkways.

I look through the upside-down canopy to the

silvery, shining mists beneath us and wonder how long I would fall before hitting the bottom.

I feel a sudden sense of vertigo.

I'm afraid of heights, you know—or I used to be, long ago. The trick is to learn to like it. The trick is to be exhilarated by the fear. I feel it now, the exhilaration. The blood rushing through my veins. Even the air smells sweeter, somehow. It smells like . . . something, a lost memory.

Like cut grass.

Jesus fucking Christ, it smells like freshly cut grass. I breathe in and let the air out slowly.

Then I sneeze.

Fuck, I forgot about that part.

Aiden's step is unsteady, and I start to worry he might fall. El Cid must have seen it, too, because she helps strap him onto Q.

I can tell the pain has gotten much worse for my son. He's not able to talk anymore, and murky tears are running out of his eyes. I wipe that half-wight, half-human blood off his lip again.

"Follow me," Amirani says.

"How far down is it?" I ask, watching the bright, silvery mists that roil like thunderclouds below.

Amirani frowns. "No one knows. But the devils come from there, crawling along the walls or flying up through the abyss. I led an exploratory team down a while back. The light that brightens the mist dies away a couple of hundred feet beneath the canopy. Below that, darkness. I believe the clippings and tree leaves which fall to the floor become fodder for a fungus. I believe the pigmiditz live off that fungus. Just a theory I have." He points along the fifty foot diameter trunk beside us to a walkway. "This way. Like I said, the dyitzu have been lobbing fireballs at us all morning from over there." He points across the chamber to one of the farthest trees. Even at this distance, I can see men camped out behind wicker fortifications, guns leveled at the hostage tree. "I'll keep us clear of them, mostly."

I've rarely been more careful in choosing my step. The boards creek alarmingly as we walk.

"This shit stable?" Q asks.

Amirani shrugs. "We lose a person every month or so to construction failure. So, no."

"They don't let you supervise building?" El Cid asks.

"I've been working on a few things on the Lord's tree," Amirani answers. "Mostly they have me building fortifications. It's a tougher job than you'd think, though. Earth and stone, well they move a little, but these trees, they grow much faster than anything I've built on before."

The planks look almost as if they'd been manufactured in the old world. They aren't fastened with nails however. Many are fitted together. Others are tied with little wicker vines. Those are the hardest to walk on, not just because they're loose, but because the wicker makes the surface uneven.

At least it's not snow.

It doesn't help that the main light source is below us. The more I look down, the more blinded I become.

We move onto a branch which leads toward the center of the chamber. It's maybe four feet wide at this point and getting narrower. It's been braided together with the outstretched branches of another tree. I see where some of the leaves—a few almost the size of my body, others the size of my head—have been struck by dyitzu fire.

"They've been attacking the joints," Amirani explains. "Their attacks have been getting more organized lately, and they've got some Icanitzu with them. There's been a flood of Icanitzu lately, coming upstream along the Northern Lethe."

El Cid grunts. "We may have run into some of that earlier. We were hit by a pack of dyitzu on the river that was pretty well organized."

Amirani picks his way carefully across what he'd called the joint. The path is only a foot wide, but there is a vine stretched alongside us like a rail. Infidel balance or no, Amirani keeps a hand on it. I follow his example.

"Be careful," I tell Q, worried for my son.

"Damn right I'll be careful." Q answers.

Nebuchadnezzar mutters something in German.

"Is that why Portsmouth went dark?" El Cid asks,

"Icanitzu?"

The braided branches and leaves creak under Amirani's step. "I believe so. I think they've been streaming out of the Carrion for some reason. I put a few down in their initial assaults, but they've grown more wary."

I walk onto the braided joint, keeping my hand on the vine. A great many small branches, splitting off of the main one, allowed this joining to be possible. Still, a lot of the greenery has been burnt. My foot slides an inch or so on the oily residue of the dyitzu fire. I grip the vine so hard my knuckles pop.

I pause for a moment, making sure my balance is secure.

Okay. Time to walk.

"Then again, there's been a string of cities going down lately. It's Maylay Beighlay, I think. It was a huge center for trade. Ammo doesn't flow in from the east like it used to. No joke, we've been using bows and arrows from time to time."

I finish crossing the joint and take a deep breath.

Q comes up behind me, my boy safely attached to his back. Aiden's whining slightly.

I look around. This tree isn't nearly as healthy as the last. Many of its branches are drooping, and its leaves are smaller. I'm guessing it's because they've got sinfruit vines growing all over this thing. Now I understand why a person might choose to live in

Dendra despite the fear that someday the wood beneath their feet might break away, leaving them to fall into the eternal void below.

Food is a damn powerful motivator.

"This tree doesn't look so good," Q says.

Amirani nods. "The vines aren't helping, and a lot of the planks you've been walking on were harvested from this one. They're also fermenting alcohol in the trunk, which can't help. Not to mention the corpses they keep."

"Corpses?" I ask.

Then why would they be afraid of a half wight? Hypocrites.

"The corpsedust is what ferments the alcohol," Amirani answers.

Alcohol. Another good reason to live here.

"You sure there's not a Minotaur involved with those Icanitzu?" El Cid asks as we wind our way around a walkway staked into the gnarled trunk.

Amirani shrugs. "Could be. I hear the Well isn't doing so hot. That city might be something a Minotaur would strike at. Still, it would be an awfully convoluted strategy."

"The Archdevil in Maylay Beighlay is dead." El Cid tells him.

"No shit?" Amirani seems surprised at the news. "Who got him? Did Ares come out of the Carrion or something?"

El Cid shakes her head. "That fucker." She points a thumb at me. "Q's been grooming him."

Amirani's eyebrows rise. "My regards," Amirani says.

I nod at him.

There is another group of people coming toward us. They're dressed in the same brown fabric as the guards, but lack the wicker helmets. They stand to one side, allowing us to make our way carefully around them. One is a girl, and she smells nice . . . like tree sap.

It occurs to me, as I edge by them on this precarious walkway, that this is a place where you really have to trust your neighbor . . . and not piss off your wife.

Amirani waits for us to get a bit of distance from that crew before he speaks again. "So what really brings you out here?" He asks in a low voice. "I can't imagine you're actually escorting Nebuchadnezzar."

I see a trio of women a few branches above us with wicker baskets slung around their waists. They're picking sinfruit off of the vines. God I'm hungry. I wonder if they smell like tree sap, too. Particularly the busty one in the middle. You'd think Myla would have put me off of redheads, but apparently not. I guess I've got a type.

"He's got a theory on how we can cure the boy," El Cid explains quietly.

Amirani looks back for a second, eyebrows raised.

"The lad is on edge. I don't even know if Endymion can cure that."

"I don't know that I can either," Nebuchadnezzar says in his accentless voice.

Thanks for the vote of confidence, dickhead.

"We're headed to Soulfall," El Cid says, "the precipice."

Amirani whistles. "You got a plan for the Furies?"

Nebuchadnezzar grimaces. "I've got a powder that will make the Furies attack the corpses on the upper city."

"You trying to die?" Amirani asks. "That part of Hell is awful anyway. The barriers between the Carrion and there are almost gone. Devils are thick, Cid. Damn thick. Not to mention that you're actually heading to the Erebus."

"We have to try," I say.

Amirani nods. "I understand."

The fuck he does. No one understands.

We move onto an anemic looking branch which leads to the next tree.

"Heads up, here comes the Order," Amirani warns, pointing to a darkly dressed cadre of half a dozen or so men. "I guess it was too much to hope we'd avoid them."

Q gives a soft whistle.

El Cid stops in her tracks. "It's Keith."

Jesus Christ. He must be the one with the arrogant

swagger. But how did he get here before us? Unless . . .

Unless he'd guessed our plan.

"Can we go around?" Nebuchadnezzar asks.

Amirani shakes his head. "They came here to meet us. If we avoid them, they'll just move to blockade us another way. Do your best to keep them from noticing the kid. They'll take great pleasure in exposing us."

El Cid glances back over her shoulder, grimacing. "I'll distract 'em as much as I can."

"They have to know Aiden's plight already," I say. "Otherwise they wouldn't have known to come here."

El Cid's head shakes. "Maybe, but I doubt it. They might have just lucked out."

"Twice?"

She turns around and stares at me with her green eyes. The light from below and the matching color of the trees make them all the more brilliant. "I'm sorry, Cris. We may have come all this way just to lose your son now."

I shake my head. "No."

"If they set the guards against us . . ."

She points to the soldiers moving along some of the branches. "They have guns, and we don't." She turns to Amirani. "What's the punishment for leprosy?"

Amirani points down.

Jesus fucking Christ.

"And that's visited on outsiders?" she asks.

Amirani nods.

I feel rage boiling in my heart. Why did we choose to come through here?

Time. The answer was time. We have none of it.

I see the Order's people ahead of us. Five of them, standing on a platform that, unless we are to double back, we'll surely have to cross.

Our branch widens, and I move up to walk beside Cid. "Aiden lives."

"They'll give us up to the guards, Cris."

I pass her and Amirani by, heading toward Keith. "Then they all die."

Chapter 12

The men of the Order dress in a dark grey that is surprisingly close to infidel black—only they could never be mistaken for infidels. I wonder if they know how cruel their faces look. Hell, maybe they're proud of it.

The one that must be Keith steps forward as we make our way onto the platform, leaving his compatriots lounging against the trunk. He's pale, pale enough to make me think he's taking wight dust. Like Nebuchadnezzar, he looks like an American hero, but in a different way. Keith looks like a slender superman, curly black hair, blue eyes, and a dimpled chin on a strong jaw.

A few brown-clad natives are watching. They're safe enough, I suppose, since all of us have been stripped of our weapons.

"Nebuchadnezzar," Keith says with a smile on his lips, "you've gone turncoat. Did the Infidel himself pay you a visit in your snowy little tower, or was it this little cunt that turned you to the dark side?"

"Keith," Nebuchadnezzar addresses the man, "the Infidel did indeed come to my home."

There is a moment of pause. The men leaning against the tree shift awkwardly.

That's one thing I've learned about Hell. Everyone fears the Infidel. Humans, devils, doesn't matter. I've never even seen him, and *I'm* starting to fear him.

They recover quickly though, and Keith takes a couple of long looks at Q and Aiden.

"Your kind doesn't come this far west," Keith says, his eyes still on my son. "What's the occasion?"

Nebuchadnezzar grins right back at him with that damn smile which touches his eyes. "We're going to drop into the Carrion. Meet up with Ares. See how many of you poor bastards he's killed already."

Keith chuckles. "I don't fear that Neanderthal. And I don't buy your bullshit. I think you're here because it's a half-day walk to the Northern Lethe if you go around Dendra. I think you're headed to Portsmouth."

I get the feeling he's lying. I think he knows exactly what our plan is.

Q gives them a golf clap. "You'd be right. Congratulations, you figured it out."

"Shut up, nigger," Keith says. "I wasn't talking to you."

His men chuckle a bit, even the black one.

Just like with Nebuchadnezzar, Q doesn't flinch. He doesn't even look angry.

One of Keith's men, one of the cancer, leans forward off of the tree trunk. He takes a couple of steps forward. "That nigger got a monkey on his back. A dead monkey."

Oh, they ain't getting my son. Fuck them. I'm an infidel, so maybe I'm supposed to hate them already—hell, they even called my best friend a nigger—but if they want to fuck with my son . . .

I give out a short laugh.

They look at me.

"The Infidel is coming here," I say.

Keith's eyebrows rise in disbelief. El Cid watches me closely.

"Really?" Keith smiles knowingly.

I nod. "Because he knows what's at the bottom of that pit, and he knows how to clear it out. Who else do you think could get the Tree Lord to let a leper in his city?"

That shuts them up.

Hell, it was the best lie I could come up with. No time to stop now, they might think about my lie and figure it out. "And you think you're scared shitless now, staring at three infidels who don't have their weapons. Wait until you're looking at *the* Infidel. Ain't nobody taking his guns away. I bet you'll feel naked as fuck."

I see a line of guards moving along the tree to the right. At first I think they're coming this way, but then I notice they're carrying our gondola. Oh, hell, those poor bastards. Carrying that thing over the joints has got to be scary as shit.

"Sorry, Keith," El Cid says, pointing to the boat, "we've got a ride to catch. I hope you follow us, I really hope you do."

Keith sneers. "I'll see if I can't oblige you, miss."

We walk by them. I keep my body between Keith and my son, just in case.

They watch us go with cold eyes.

"Well I'm fucked," Amirani says when we make it to the next bridge. "They'll check with the Lord about the wight, and then I'll have to defend myself."

"Won't be a problem," I say.

"Oh?"

"The guard who checked us in, he'd be in some serious shit if he was caught letting a leper through, yeah?"

"He would," Amirani says.

"Lie. Say the boy was just injured and lost some blood. He'll back you up, and make them look like idiots."

Amirani smiles. "I hope that works. I'll see if we can't lock them up for it, at least for a couple days. I might be able to keep them off your trail." He stops and cocks his head, regarding me. "Where'd you find this guy?" he asks Cid.

"Find him?" Cid snorts. "This damn stray found me."

Chapter 13

It doesn't look like the guards at Dendra have stolen any of my stuff.

We'd climbed the trunk of one tree and walked up through a hollowed out root to get to the Northern Lethe. We'd left as quickly as possible, not wanting to be followed by the Order or be caught by a guard with Aiden.

The caves surrounding this river are completely natural in formation, and the lighting is very dim. Even so, the waters are wide, slow and shallow, allowing us to continue poling our way toward the Erebus.

"Keith's like a damn bad habit," Q says from the back of the gondola.

"He knows," I say.

"Knows what?"

"Everything." I pause while Q brings us around a rock, noticing that everyone, even Aiden, is listening to me. "What we're doing. Where we're going. The state that Aiden's in."

Q frowns. "That's impossible."

"Can you think of anything else that would explain how he's been able to follow us so closely? He even beat us to Dendra. Unless he knows a faster route than we do, he must have taken his men straight from the Pole to Dendra even before we saw Nebuchadnezzar."

El Cid says nothing, but her eyes are on me and me alone. Her lips are slightly parted. Suddenly, for some reason I can't quite explain, I feel nervous.

Q shakes his head. "He's not psychic, Cris. It has to be luck. Maybe they know a faster way or heard from the Pole natives that we were going down the river."

El Cid is still looking at me, and I think her cheeks are slightly flushed.

"Durgan," I say.

Q's eyes narrow, and he looks at me for a moment before returning his attention to the river. "Who?"

"You said there was a wight with Keith. I know who it is. It's Durgan. He's one of, well, *was* one of the Archdevil's wights. I never killed him. He'd know exactly what state Aiden is in."

"But to anticipate our travel to Dendra," Q says, "he'd have to know more than that. He'd have to know our solution. And unless that Creature or Jeeves is talking—"

"Hansel," Nebuchadnezzar corrects.

"Whatever," Q says, annoyed. "So unless that Creature or *Jeeves* is talking, there's no way they'd know we're headed to the Erebus."

"I'm not so sure," Cid's voice is soft, but we all shut up and look to her. "The Order is deeply connected to the City of Blood and Stone. Lucreas Crassus has been a key player in both. It's possible that Keith knows enough about wights, with the help of Durgan, to have guessed our next move."

Q frowns, and I can see him reconsidering my position. "Maybe. I wouldn't bet on it, but maybe."

"Half a day, then," El Cid says, her eyes still boring into me.

"What do you mean?" I ask.

"If Durgan is with them, then we have a half day lead."

Something clicks in my head, and I realize what she's saying. "Because if Durgan is with

them, they won't be able him through Dendra, so if they're going to follow us, they'll have to go around. And that's a half day journey."

El Cid's smiles, her lips parting a little farther.

Q poles us around another bend. "Hopefully we'll never find out for sure."

We go on in silence, and after a few hours, I drift off to sleep.

Q and Cid wake me so they can get some rest.

Aiden is napping, so that means my only company is Nebuchadnezzar . . . and any devils that might be around.

"Any devilsign?" I ask.

The necromancer shakes his blond head. "No, and El Cid said it would be a few more hours before things get dangerous. Dendra sends out people to gather along this river, and apparently they keep the devils clear of it."

"So what changed your mind?" I ask.

He looks at me, apparently unsure of what I was asking him.

"I mean, you're not a Nazi anymore."

Nebuchadnezzar stares into the cold waters from where he stands on the back of the gondola. He glances at Cid, but she's dead asleep.

"The Infidel," his accentless voice intones.

"Of course, the Infidel, but what did he *say*?"

Nebuchadnezzar lifts the pole out of the water and braces it against a rock to keep us clear of it. The current pulls us on, gently, inexorably, toward the river of darkness.

"One fact and one irony."

"I'm listening."

"Well, first he told me about hybrid vigor. The idea of a master race isn't as compelling after you know genetic diversity makes for healthier humans."

"And the irony?" I ask.

"Yeah. You see, we could sense that we were on the brink of a new era. We knew that this was the one time in history where a minute technological advantage would have megalithic consequences. We knew it would assure victory to one side—only we didn't know under which rock that victory lay. We were ahead of you in all technologies. In rockets, years ahead. In jets, we had two jet planes out while you and your allies were fiddling with prop engines. We were ahead in tanks, in submarines, in battleships . . . in everything. Everything—except for one thing. We were behind in nuclear weapons. Do you know why?"

I remember it being something about heavy water, but I don't know the details. "No."

Nebuchadnezzar's Aryan eyes settle on me. "When the Nazi Party came to power, they weren't strong enough, or sure enough, or hateful enough, to start with the concentration camps right away. But even before we opened the ghettos, we began removing Jews from powerful and prestigious positions. Step by step, little by little. We did it to gypsies, too, and others, but mostly Jews. We did it in all walks of life, in little baby steps. In our government, in our businesses, and in our Universities. In the Universities we moved the Jewish faculty away from the most respected positions. Positions like engineering. But in the beginning we didn't fire them, we just put them in shitty little jobs. There was this field that was not well respected, you see. Theoretical particle physics. And the Jews we moved into that field, they studied the shit out of it. Then they defected. Their research became the basis of

Oppenhiemer's work. You got the bomb from German research. The Infidel, he said to me that if somehow Germany had been able to build that Reich, not on the back of hatred, but with something else—with something that didn't sacrifice a part of our culture—that we would have been able to win that race, and with the V rockets, the war. At the time he said that to me, I didn't think a society could be built up from the ashes like Germany had been without a scapegoat. Now, however, I'm not so sure."

I let my hand trail in the water for a moment. "But here, it's possible. I mean, we can have hate for the devils. We could build a society like that."

"You know why I'm not an Infidel Friend?" he asks.

I am curious about that. "Why?"

"Because the Infidel came to me and gave me an argument and an offer. The argument worked, but he has nothing I want." Nebuchadnezzar's voice seems strangely angry.

This might be the first time I've seen him rattled. "What did he offer you?"

"He said he could take away the guilt I feel at being part of them. But I don't feel guilt, you see. We were straddling the line between the old world and the new. Between a genocide hating modernity and a genocide accepting past. We didn't know about hybrid vigor, you see. We really thought that they weren't of *us*. So I don't need to have guilt. I was doing the best I could."

He guides us around some rocks. "There are some things that are both right and counter-intuitive, you see," he goes on. "You might have to hurt someone you love to stop them from committing murder. You can't just follow your gut. There was this girl who had the prettiest brown eyes. I didn't want to start cutting them open. I didn't. She asked if I was married while she was waiting. She hadn't eaten in some time. I could count her ribs. She told me not to worry, that I'd find someone someday. And I felt in my gut that I shouldn't hurt her. But I knew the feeling was wrong. If I could just get her eyes to be blue then . . ."

Our hull scrapes against some rocks as we pass by them.

"Did she die?" I ask.

"No, I didn't kill her. She's not dead. Just blind. Just blind."

I'm no angel. Hell, I killed twenty innocent workers so I could murder Aiden's mother, but I sure as hell wouldn't want that weight on my shoulders.

"Neb, I think when this shit is done, and before we go looking for Eva, maybe we should get you to the Infidel."

"I told you, I don't feel guilty."

"Maybe not," I say. "Maybe you really are a fucking monster."

He snorts.

"Was she right?" I ask.

"Who?"

"The little girl, was she right that there was a woman out there for you?"

"Cris, that girl thought I was a nice doctor. I don't think she was a very good judge of those kinds of things."

But maybe she was. What if there was some truth to the bullshit he was slinging at me? What if what caused this man to be so evil was just a set of bad ideas? Could a few misconceptions be so powerful? Or were there worse genocides in store for humanity, ones that were made all the more terrible by the fact that their perpetrators knew exactly what they were doing?

Chapter 14

"**Cris**," El Cid's soft voice cuts through my dreams. "I'm sorry, sweetheart. Wake up."

Sweetheart? She's calling me that now?

I'd managed to sleep a bit more comfortably this time. Even so, I feel like shit. It's like I woke up, but the center of my chest didn't. Aiden's shaking in my arms, on the edge of consciousness, kept there no doubt by his pain.

"How soon until we can medicate him?" I ask.

El Cid's eyebrows arch. "Can't understand you, you're words are slurred."

I shake my head to clear it. "How soon until we can give him the ferment?"

Her face is grim. "We've got trouble." She looks at Aiden, and for a moment I think she's going to cry.

Nebuchadnezzar pulls us against one of the natural embankments of the Northern Lethe. Hell's architect has left these caverns all but untouched. A stalactite splits the river ahead of us, making the tunnel almost look like the inside of a cartoon mouth.

"Why are we stopping?" I ask.

Aiden gives another whimper.

El Cid holds a finger over her mouth.

Okay, darling, I'll shut up. But not for long.

The boat rocks a little as El Cid hops onto the shore.

I set Aiden's head down gently against the edge of the boat. He's cold. Damn cold. Colder than a human can be. I kiss him on the forehead. Q holds the gondola steady against the shore as I sit on the bank and crawl to my feet. He follows me, his long limbs letting him step out of the boat with a single stride.

I look back.

Nebuchadnezzar, necromancer and Nazi, stands guard over my boy. He holds the craft still with the pole.

Cid and Q pull me to the base of a stalagmite and huddle with me there.

"What's up?" I ask.

"Sorry we had to pull you out of the boat," El Cid says. "We couldn't trust you to keep your cool."

The light coming from the water is blue, and it's got her face half in shadow. Sometimes I forget how beautiful El Cid can be.

I look to Q.

"He's slipping." Q says.

No way. He's been off the ferment. "I can't believe that. He's been so strong. He held up, without medication, the entire time in Dendra."

El Cid nods. "Nebuchadnezzar noticed it first. Aiden's off balance. He's no longer on edge. He's just a few hours away from becoming a wight."

"But he faced the pain!" I insist. "He should be *more* alive."

Cid frowns. Her green eyes seem blue in this lighting. She looks to the floor. "All my training, everything I've learned about Hell says that we should cut our losses. That we should leave."

"No," I hear my voice crack on the word. "We came all this way. We did everything right. We did . . ."

Infidels don't cry.

They had done everything right. Not me. I knew Myla was going bad before she left me. I knew some of the things she'd taught Aiden were evil. But I tried to compromise. I thought I had to. But I was weak. If I'd known, I could have taken him away then. Or at least not let her teach him that garbage. Then he wouldn't have gone with her. Or he would have had the right mindset to resist becoming a wight.

I'd hit him, once.

Is it any wonder he wants to die? It's a miracle that he ever loved me. Maybe God knew what he was doing when he sent me to Hell. I was never cut out to be a father. I was never mature enough. I could never take responsibility for myself. Hell, in the old world, I couldn't even take care of a pet. What the Hell was I doing, thinking I could have a kid?

Infidels don't cry. Fathers don't cry. If Aiden sees me, he'll lose strength. I've done him enough wrong already.

I feel sick. I kneel down. I'm struggling for air.

"Cris," El Cid says.

I think she's been talking to me. I just haven't been hearing her.

I prepare my voice because I know I won't be able to speak right. "What?" I choke.

"It's not over."

I look up at her. Infidels don't cry.

I pinch the bridge of my nose and close my eyes tightly. "It's not?" I feel the tears pushing out against all my efforts.

"I'll scout Portsmouth," Q says.

El Cid shakes her head. "No time."

I feel Q shift above me. "But you said we'd be damned before you went into Portsmouth cold."

"I'm giving him something other than ferment, Cris. It'll slow him down, way down. He'll be a log. He might even die. He really might, but before he does, the progress of the wightflesh will slow."

I nod, and with shaky legs, regain my feet.

"We'll go through Portsmouth cold," El Cid says. "With Aiden knocked out, we'll ride the river to the edge and try and drop down into Soulfall. It's not the best way, but it's the fastest. I'll give you a hungerleaf wrap when we get close. It's like taking an amphetamine, it will keep you awake. The last thing we want, Cris, is to come up to the Erebus tired. The closer our minds are to dreaming, the more shit we'll be in."

"I'll stay awake," I say.

"You will," she says, "for three days. We're heading into some thick shit here. We're out of Dendra's protective bubble. Devils migrate up out of the Carrion along the Erebus. We won't be able to afford any time to sleep."

I'm about to collapse now.

"Three days," Q says.

I nod. "Three days."

El Cid takes a couple of steps back to the boat. She stops, turns around, and offers me a hand. I take it, and she leads me back to the gondola.

She stands there on the bank, and I use her hand to balance myself as I get in. I start to pull away, but Cid hasn't let go.

"Three days," she says, "and Aiden lives."

Chapter 15

"This isn't working," Cid says.

She's got one foot on the side of the raised prow, one hand resting gently on the Chinese dragon's neck and the other on her chin.

My heart sinks.

A stalactite seems like it's about to hit her in the head. She doesn't flinch and the thing passes by so close to her that it draws back a few strands of her hair.

I don't know if I have the energy to contradict her. And here I'd thought she'd finally come to my side.

"You said . . ." I begin, but when she turns around, I question myself.

Her tiny, angry face fills me with a mixture of hope and lust. From this angle, with her half turned, I can see the ever-so-slight push of her small bust against her body armor. Maybe it's the fact that I'm about to pass out with exhaustion, but I want nothing more than to fuck her right now. Her green eyes are narrowed, and there's a flush in her normally pale cheeks.

Q looks up from where he sits, and even

Nebuchadnezzar stops poling for a second.

She turns back to stare at the long dark waterway. "Q, hand out some hungerleaf wraps to keep us awake. Then get the oars."

Q cocks his head to one side. "We're going as fast as we can, Cid. The devils, we need to be able to adjust to each new room."

She turns and grins. "We don't have time for that, Q. Our speed will surprise them, certainly."

Nebuchadnezzar seems like he's about to say something, but for once, the Nazi keeps his God damned mouth shut.

"We're close to Portsmouth," Q says. "We should be careful going through there at least."

El Cid lets her hand fall to her pistol, then shakes her head. "We've been warned of Icanitzu. I've loaded the stone shells. Get me speed, Q. You and Neb and Cris will cycle off."

"You too good to row?" Nebuchadnezzar asks.

I knew his silence wouldn't last.

She grins. "Too good a shot, yes, unless you want to pick the Icanitzu off?"

For a moment I think he's going to argue with her, but Hell, he hasn't had any more sleep than the rest of us.

Q hands me a small thing wrapped in a dark green hungerleaf. "We'll take more after we start to crash," he says, meeting my eyes. "But after you've had three, they'll do more harm than good."

He passes one to El Cid and another to Nebuchadnezzar before swallowing his own. I lay it on my tongue. It's as bitter as copper. Hell, the taste itself is enough to keep me awake. I feel my heart come to life. My drooping eyes snap back open. I feel alive, strangely alive, as if the awareness is just pasted on top of where I was exhausted before—but I'll take it. The air, cooled from the river below us, feels good as I breathe it in.

Fuck. I feel ready.

How long has it been since I've felt this way?

Q's first paddle strokes hit the river. I hear the rippling of the water. The boat creaks as he leans forward. In all things the infidels are technical. His oars hit the river again at the exact moment he's completed his forward motion. Then his torso shoots back, and the oars cut through the water. Our boat picks up a little more speed.

Stroke.

And a little more.

Stroke.

And a little more.

El Cid is still at the prow, the loose strands of her hair whipping around her head. She undoes the black silk strip she uses in her hair and, after her fingers coax the loose strands back in line, she re-ties it.

The Northern Lethe, as if sensing our need, joins with another waterway, becomes deeper and picks up speed—working with Q to power us toward the Erebus.

Stroke.

And we're moving a little faster.

Stroke.

And a little faster.

Azure skystone runs through these chambers, giving us all a deep greenish-blue cast. As we pass beneath low archways from cavern room to cavern room, the skystone veins seem to disappear—except for those in the riverbed.

The rush of the water and the cut of our boat causes the aquamarine light to oscillate over the shadow-pocked stone ceilings, distant cubbyholes and corridors. I see our wake as evidenced by the ripples of the light on the rock roof behind us.

Oh, Hell, you are so beautiful. And just like I despised Myla, I fucking hate your guts for it.

"Faster," El Cid orders.

Q's intensity increases.

Stroke. Stroke. Stroke.

El Cid shoulders her M-16. I draw the Old Lady. Neb pulls out a Luger from his overcoat.

Chapter 16

Q propels us into a small cavern. Two dyitzu spot us, their black eyes shining in the rippling aquamarine light. We're halfway through the room before I fell one with the Old Lady—the shotgun blast is deafening in the tight confines. El Cid lets the other stand. It tosses fire after us, but a deft stutter paddle from Q keeps us clear of the missile.

And then we're gone.

I kneel by Aiden and prop him up against the side of the gondola in a way that seems, to me at least, like it would be more comfortable. I check him for breath to make sure he's alive.

He is. Just barely, but he is.

"It's okay, son. Cid's going to take care of us."

Stroke. Stroke. Stroke.

Our next caverns are larger, more spacious, and their ceilings soar over us. The ripples of the water make each room seem alive with enemies, even if they are completely empty. My head jerks back and forth as the shadows play on the edges of my vision.

Then I see a devil climbing up along the ceiling. It's maybe three feet tall, winged, and with golden skin. I hope like hell this thing can't throw fire.

The infidels call them pigmiditz, or pigs for short. I just call them imps.

"Heads up!" El Cid calls.

I realize that the ceiling is covered with them. They're crawling upside down like little exorcist babies, trying to get over us. El Cid lights up the room with three-round bursts and the imps start falling like rain.

"Faster!" Cid yells.

Stroke.

The first one I spotted drops from the ceiling and lands right on the stern of the gondola, a foot away from Neb's head. The Nazi shrieks.

Stroke.

I lean forward, getting the Old Lady within point blank range so that stray buckshot doesn't kill the Aryan necromancer before his time, and fire. Its shoulder and face explode as its body topples backward.

Stroke.

Its corpse hits the water to join the splashes of the ones El Cid is killing.

Neb shakes off the panic and starts firing.

Stroke.

They're dropping all around us now and not all of them are dead. They start swimming toward us, heads bobbing like rats. I see one as a silhouette against the azure light of the river, a foot or so under water. It spreads its wings and launches itself up through the surface, droplets glinting in the light, heading right for Cid's back.

With a quick shift, I launch a volley of buckshot at it—mutilating it. The creature hits Cid, but bounces off of her, falling into the water on the far side. Cid turns with the hit and fires. And fires again. She switches clips so fast I can barely detect the extra pause between her shots.

A trio of imps plummet dead to the stone bank, one after another. I hear Nebuchadnezzar take a shot with his Luger. The hollow sound of the Nazi weapon fills the chamber as a fourth imp falls, crashing into the river.

More are coming at us, darting through the water.

"Neb!" I yell. "Below!"

I switch my grip on the Old Lady as a wave of golden imps breaches the surface, rocketing up toward us.

Nebuchadnezzar shoots one down as I Babe Ruth another. El Cid ducks the third which sails over us. The necromancer holsters his Luger and picks up the pole.

Two more waves come. Neb and I knock them down as El Cid pivots about, shooting the imps on the ceiling closest to us. One, flailing after taking a round to the chest, bounces off the edge of our boat before falling into the water.

We're almost out of this room. As the imps lunge toward us, they fill the air with a fine mist. The cool water is invigorating.

I hit another with the butt of the Old Lady and droplets of black devil blood joins the spray and coats my face. It tastes different than human blood. It's bitter, and like the hungerleaf wrap, it makes me feel alive.

El Cid fires one more round as we enter the tunnel.

Stroke. Stroke. Stroke.

Shells, blood and one dead imp lay at the base of our boat. I pick up a shell, still hot, off of my son and toss it aside. Neb uses the pole as a lever to flip the tiny devil corpse out of the gondola.

Stroke. Stroke. Stroke.

The next room is larger, stretching almost half a mile. The river here widens into a lake. The light seems a tinge more green, and it barely touches the domed ceiling which hovers some three hundred yards above us. Along the shore, over the ruins of a fallen stone city, and all along that domed ceiling, the imps see us.

I feel no dread.

Q laughs.

"Faster." El Cid's breathy voice makes my blood boil.

Stroke, stroke, stroke.

A horde of the imps dive into the water as we speed toward the center of the lake. The ceiling is crawling with them, like an army of evil three foot golden roaches climbing to intercept us.

"Schaben," Neb says, blue eyes narrowed, the nostrils on his Roman nose flaring.

I've no clue what the fuck he just said, but I know I agree with the sentiment.

Chapter 17

Jesus those fuckers are swimming fast. I see ripples in the water on the far side of the lake where they are leaving the shore en masse. That disturbance in the water, and the golden shadowlike figures beneath the surface, are coming at us with the speed of a runner's sprint.

"What did you say?" I ask Q loudly over the rush of the air and sound of his rowing.

"The ceiling." Q's breathing heavy. "They've got enough space to glide."

Shit, they can glide?

Stroke, stroke, stroke.

"More of them than we have bullets," El Cid says. "Q, where's your fire?"

Infidel Fire. The one thing the infidel's ridiculously scientific world view gives them is a good understanding of how to warp the materials of Hell into an explosive. Still, even for them, it's hard as hell to make the stuff, and if Cid wants to use it, that means she thinks we'll die without it.

"My pack," Q answers, "right pocket, near the bottom."

El Cid leans down and fishes out two metal cylinders, each about six inches long and maybe two inches thick. She tucks them into a pocket sewn into the back of her body armor.

She shoulders her M-16 as I fill the Old Lady with shells.

There are so many climbing along the ceiling ahead of us that it looks almost like they are a molten gold river flowing upside down. The part of the lake beneath them is smooth enough that I can see the reflection of that river in the glowing water.

"Edge right, Q," El Cid orders. "We need more space between us and the swimmers."

"Longer route!" Q warns, nearly breathless.

"I know," Cid says.

Stroke, stroke, stroke.

One of the imps along the ceiling drops. I watch it plummet. Is it dead? No, Q warned me that they glide.

After falling about a third of the way to the lake, perhaps one hundred yards, it throws out its small wings. The imp's descent curves, leveling off almost completely as it soars toward us.

"Gott im Himmel," Nebuchadnezzar breathes.

It's as if that first imp's flight was a signal. They start coming in droves, dropping from the ceiling like the rain of some biblical plague. A few spread their wings early, others later, but they are all heading in our direction.

I realize that this is probably the end.

El Cid starts firing. I join her. We kill dozens, but there are so many.

"Faster, Q!" El Cid shouts over a pair of three-round bursts. "As fast as you can. Straight to the exit."

Stroke-stroke-stroke.

El Cid lets her M-16 fall into the boat and draws her thin, white sword from her pack. Q's blade handle is sticking out of his.

It's as if he reads my mind because he shouts. "Get it, Cris!"

The head of the imp wave is two hundred feet away.

I draw the purple-bladed weapon.

One hundred fifty.

El Cid draws a canister of infidel fire, not one of Q's, from a holster where she keeps her sawed-off double barrel. She throws it, not toward the flying throng, but ahead and to the left of the boat. Toward the swimmers that will reach us first.

One hundred feet.

The cylinders have a vacuum tube inside them which draws in the air when their seal is broken. I hear that as a high pitched whistle while the cylinder flies. Will it even work if it hits the lake?

It splashes amidst the golden horde . . . and then

explodes. Water shoots up into the air. It's not just the swimmers right by the blast which are affected. For some reason, the imps for thirty feet or so all stop swimming.

She's already thrown a second cylinder.

And then Q's pair.

Their whistles mix together, each at a slightly different pitch.

One explodes midair, filling the sky with fire and sending the imps careening in all directions. Two more detonate in the water, almost directly in front of us. Great geysers of blood colored misty water rise up from the lake.

Q rows us into the falling droplets.

The imps, blinded by the geyser but guided by instinct, come bursting through the mist. El Cid is striking already, adding their blood to the rain. The white and purple glow of our weapons overpowers the azure color of the skystone beneath us.

I slice one out of the air as Neb starts firing his Luger.

One crashes into me, knocking me down over my comatose son. Its beaked mouth tears through my shirt, puncturing the skin at my shoulder. El Cid's white blade flicks over, cutting through the imp's skull.

The water rains down on me as I regain my footing on the rocking boat.

Stroke-stroke-stroke.

Suddenly we're clear of the mist. Most of them have overshot us. I see them through the haze, dropping into the water. The swimmers are behind us now and gaining. El Cid draws another pair of infidel fire cylinders.

"We'll be out!" Q warns.

El Cid nods and tosses one behind us.

Again, a whistle fills the cavern. The imps swim on, heedless of the explosive. As before, the blast is far more effective than I'd imagine. Even those devils fifty or sixty feet away, while not killed or stopped, seem to swim slower.

The water pressure, I realize. It's like fishing with dynamite.

She holds the last cylinder for a moment, but it's clear they'll catch up with us. She throws it straight up. I watch it fall behind us as Q rows onward.

This whistle seems lower than the rest.

Another geyser.

The lake, once smooth, is covered in ripples and waves. The azure light on the ceiling oscillates madly. The next wave of swimmers draws near. I join Neb at the back, sword brandished.

"Shotgun!" El Cid yells.

Neb loads another clip into his Luger. Fuck the Old Lady, I've got to conserve shells.

They come leaping up out of the water at us. The Luger picks two off. I slash another out of the sky, Q's blade ripping into its wing. They keep coming. I slash madly as Neb shoots them down.

Suddenly, so quickly I almost fall over, the open air above us disappears as we enter a low ceilinged cave. I duck down instinctively. We've made it to the exit tunnel. Neb shoots down another pair of imps. I stand back up and slash a third.

I peer into the water as the gondola races forward.

"You can slow down now, Q," El Cid says.

Stroke.

I turn. El Cid is standing, legs spread, over my boy. Dead imps, and parts of imps, litter the boat.

Stroke.

We're still going faster than is safe, but it's no longer the mad sprint Q kept us at in the lake.

I lean down, checking Aiden. He'd slept through the whole thing. An imp hand lies on his belly. I toss it out of the boat and check his breath.

He's still alive.

I open one of his eyelids. God, his eyes are so dark I can barely see the blue.

I sheath Q's weapon and help Cid with the blood and the bodies.

Stroke.

"Neb," El Cid says, picking up a still twitching imp, "spell Q for a bit."

Q shakes his head. "I'm good."

She tosses the imp corpse into the river. Its lifeless

body floats after us for a while.

Q's endurance is unbelievable. I didn't know a man could row that fast for so long, let alone keep us moving afterward.

El Cid looks at me.

She must be thinking that we'll die doing this.

I don't mind death, personally. This is something I have to do, but it's not her fight. She shouldn't die here. It's not *her* son.

"I'm sorry," I tell her. "I'm sorry you might die here for a boy that isn't yours."

"I told you," she says, "you'll make it up to me."

Chapter 18

When I was a child, I awoke from a nightmare that had seemed to last for years. This is the same—except it's no dream.

I have no way of measuring time. In the beginning, I could remember how many turns I'd taken at the oars, but that was long ago. All I know now is that my arms are dead at my sides—burning with pain.

We've run out of ammunition. I was the first, but not the last. That honor went to Q, probably because he was rowing during the imp attack at Portsmouth.

As we journey deeper into Hell, the devils seem more surprised. Perhaps they've never seen a human before. Sometimes we can even get through a devil-filled room fast enough to avoid being attacked.

Sometimes.

Without bullets, it's difficult to fend off the dyitzu. We rely on the rower, whose spent arms are expected to speed us away from danger.

Aiden remains still through it all. He barely breathes. I keep hoping he'll arise from his slumber, but maybe I shouldn't wish for that. Maybe the next time he opens his eyes, they'll be all black.

The river draws us onward, and the farther we go, the darker the shadows at the edge of my vision become. I'm hypnotized by the irregularly shaped cavern walls, by the smooth pull of the water, and when it's my turn at the oars, by the methodical agony of the beat of my strokes.

At first I think the shadows are growing because Hell is getting darker—and maybe it is—but when I look into the gondola, it's as if there is a film over my eyes, dimming the visage of my son.

"I need another of those wraps," I say, my voice dry and hoarse.

Q shakes his head.

"I'm about to tip over, Q." I'm not lying.

I'm sitting on one of the wooden benches, my useless arms hanging between my knees, my head bowed.

"You can't," Q says. "You've had three already."

Is that true? I don't remember having another after the second one. Or was that the third, and I forgot the second? Who cares? It doesn't matter.

The boat slows as Nebuchadnezzar's strokes become less frequent.

"My turn," Q says.

El Cid stops him.

"You're point," Q insists, "you've got to . . ."

She ignores him and takes a seat at the oars.

It's the right decision. None of us can row for very long anymore. In the distance I hear a banshee scream. It's not a comforting sound.

"She's coming for us," I say.

Nebuchadnezzar peers behind us, his blue irises standing out against his bloodshot eyes and the black circles which surround them. He seems more pale than usual. His, like mine, arms hang down limply by his sides. They must also be useless. The Nazi knows my pain, and I know his.

None of us are very alert. Someone has to watch.

I want to stand up to keep an eye on our surroundings. It doesn't happen. Instead my head lolls to one side as the riverbank passes smoothly by. Here the stones are grey in color, volcanic rock I'd bet, and they're pockmarked with tiny holes.

They remind me of the pattern buckshot leaves in a body.

Past the grey pitted rocks is a smoother kind of stone. It had been a river of lava once, I'm guessing, before solidifying. Part of that stream touches our river where a mound of volcanic looking stone rises.

Beyond that room crystals appear in the ceilings and in the walls. The light of the river is now a dark green, and the deeper we get, the darker the green becomes. Then some of the skystone turns orange. The ripples in the water make the stones look like they're burning.

God, are you here? Can you hear me? Is it possible for you to hear anyone in Hell? Would you even want to?

Let me tell you something, God. What I'm about to say comes from the heart, not like when your Christians pray. I don't know why you like them. They're a dishonest people. Not dishonest because they tell things they think are untrue. Not because they aren't trying to be earnest, or loving, or full of compassion. They are liars because they fooled themselves first. They took a wire in their brain and jammed it in the wrong hole. They're dead eyed, like a pot head, but with more credulity than a man can stomach. Fools. You want to be worshiped by fools? Why? But that's not what I want to tell you. I want to tell you what I'm saying means more because this is what I honestly want to say. It comes from a man who didn't sabotage his own brain or build up stupidity in some reservoir. It comes from a man who has the will to make his own decisions. From someone who doesn't ask your help or guidance for his every life choice. From a man who's brave enough to judge you.

So listen carefully.

We shouldn't have to eat to live. We shouldn't have needs. We shouldn't have the power to hurt each other. Why did you give us that? What kind of bullshit was that? I understand why the Devil did, but you? You were supposed to be the good one. Isn't that negligence? Isn't that like leaving a child alone in a house with a loaded gun? Isn't that like leaving someone in an Eden with a tasty self-destruct switch? Isn't that like, not that I'm the best parent here, leaving your child alone in a street when he calls for your help.

You were willing to let your son die for you? Well fuck you. I'm dying for my son. You got that one backward.

Devil? Are you there? You fell from heaven to create a place of torture? Or was it torturous before you got here? What happened to taking the moral high ground? This place could be an Eden? Right? Couldn't it—with a little redecorating?

Aiden whimpers and suddenly I'm filled with energy. I reach down into the cold rushing water, dodge El Cid's metronomic oar swing, and splash water into my face.

"I was nodding off," I report.

El Cid doesn't respond.

I pick up the Old Lady from my pack and lay her across my lap. She's just a club now, but she's all I've got left.

Aiden whimpers again. I put a hand to his head. It's hot, burning up. My heart beats faster.

Stroke.

"El Cid," I say.

She doesn't answer.

Stroke.

"I just wanted to tell you . . ."

Stroke.

" . . . that I love you."

The boat glides forward, tugged on by the river.

She picks up the oars and puts them inside the boat. She turns and looks at me. I realize now that we're the only ones awake. This deep into Hell, Cid had said, it isn't safe to have people sleeping.

We need to wake the others.

Far behind us, farther off than before, the banshee calls.

"You are willful and reckless," El Cid says. "You use your passion and anger to bully others into doing what's best for you, into accomplishing your desires. You think you know everything, that you have all the answers, but really, your mind is just making things up on the edges of your knowledge. When those falsities are confronted, you don't give them up easily."

Something's wrong.

What she's saying shouldn't bother me so much, but I guess the part of my brain which is supposed to protect me from such insults is asleep. I start crying. Infidels don't cry, but what right do I have to call myself an infidel?

Yet, when I see Cid there, in all her green-eyed glory, I find that I'm not mad at her. I still love her.

"I love you," I tell her again. "Even if Aiden . . .

even if we all die, I wanted to let you know that . . ."

She smiles. "You remind me of the tale about two wolves inside a man. Compassion and Anger. Do you know which one wins?"

I nod. "The one I feed."

"Fuck no, you dumb ass. There aren't wolves inside people."

I smile.

"But I know something about you, Cris. When you're this tired, you can't help but be who you really are. All your pretensions fall away. And do you know what I've learned about your core?"

I shake my head.

El Cid ducks as a crystal covered stalactite passes by overhead. "I've learned you have good taste in women."

I laugh.

Our boat, unguided, scrapes along one stone bank for a moment before the current catches us again.

The cool air feels good on my face. "You should have seen Aiden's mother. You might not be very happy to be in that company."

El Cid smiles and looks at Aiden. "She breeds well, at least."

I feel a flush on my cheeks. "Do you always insult people right before you compliment them?"

She purses her lips. "I suppose I do."

My arms start to cramp, so I raise them, trying to

loosen them up. "Keeps people off balance, huh?"

"If you're not used to hearing the truth, Cris, yes."

She picks the oars back up.

"I'm not," I tell her.

"I know. That's what it means to spend time with us infidels. It will start to rub off on you. Then, when you meet the people who live behind walls of white lies, you'll wonder why they bothered to care if they looked fat in a dress or if their laugh was annoying. Why go to all that effort to protect yourself from bullets which aren't even aimed at you?"

I scratch my chin. "I'm not sure if I know what you're talking about."

Stroke.

And the crystal-filled caverns keep on passing by.

Stroke.

"I'm sorry, Cris." She pauses as she leans back from her oars, turning her face toward me. Our lips are only inches apart.

"Why?"

"If I had more energy, I'd tell you what I was talking about." She turns back around.

Stroke.

I watch her as she rows. I try to remember what it was she said, so I can think about what she might have meant, but I can't seem to get a handle on it. It's like a word, hovering on the tip of your tongue, waiting for you to say it—only . . .

The even rhythm of her rowing becomes the gentle percussion to the music in my mind. It's a song, distant, unfamiliar, sung by a feminine voice. It's wordless, faintly operatic.

I freeze. It's Myla's voice.

Fuck.

"Cid!" I warn her. "Cid, Myla's here."

She glances at me, her sweaty brow creased with worry. "Who?"

"Myla. My ex."

"Cris, you killed her."

I shake my head to clear it. I must be hallucinating.

El Cid puts the oars aside and listens too. "Hellsong," she whispers. "I recognize it. It's the song of devils."

"But it's *her* voice!" I insist. "And I don't know the song of devils. I can't be mishearing it!"

El Cid looks to Aiden. He's twitching with pain again.

"Wake everyone," El Cid says. "We're near the Erebus."

My hands shake as I reach for Q. "How do you know?" I ask.

"When the world becomes subjective, you can hear another's hellsong more clearly. We're hearing Aiden's now."

Neb struggles into consciousness, breathing

heavily. Q comes to more gracefully, but even he looks half-dead. The hull of our boat scrapes against the dark, natural rock of the bank. I look around the room, but I'm so tired I can't make my mind retain its features. I put my hands on the bank and try to push myself up, but my arms are so spent that I have to use my legs to help.

I roll onto the ground, ending up on my back. Q passes my pack to me. I reach out and grab it with one wet-noodle arm. The effort of climbing onto the bank has me winded. I let my head fall to one side as I wait to catch my breath.

Neb is bending the pole against the stones, leaning his weight against it. It cracks. He picks up the bigger end and swings it in the air. I'm sure it will make a good club for him.

I see faint blue flashes from a chamber ahead. The light seems to come and go along with Myla's song.

"Lights," I say.

Q is standing over me. "That's the Erebus, Cris." He reaches down, offering me a hand. "Now for the hard part."

"We're maybe a half mile downstream from Soulfall," Cid says as Q lugs me to my feet. "Go ahead and feed a wrap to Aiden. We'll need him as mobile as we can make him."

Q produces one of the wraps and offers it to my son. Thankfully, my boy is awake. He gags on it, and then stands on shaky legs. I think he's still alive, and not a wight, but it's hard as hell to tell.

"You okay?" I ask him.

His nearly black eyes focus on me. "I'll keep up."

"It'll be a few minutes before that kicks in all the way," Q says. "We'll put you on your father's back, then take you down when we reach Soulfall."

Q picks up Aiden and straps him on me. My son's even breathing tells me that he's fallen back asleep already.

"Don't worry," Q says, sensing my concern, "he'll wake back up in a few."

"Everyone got everything from the boat?" Neb asks.

"Yeah." The word barely leaves my lips.

Silently, we stand there on the bank. The gondola drifts along.

Nebuchadnezzar looks after it wistfully. "They used to bury kings like this. They'd put them in a boat and send them down the river. Then an archer would shoot a flaming arrow after it, to issue the king into the next world."

It strikes me as fitting because, if what the infidels say is right, this boat is about to go off the edge of Gehenna.

"Then who are we burying?" I ask.

Neb swallows. "Ourselves."

And then, as if to make his statement true, dyitzu

pour into our room.

"Run!" Cid yells.

I sprint for an exit.

Chapter 19

"We don't have time to stop!" Cid screams.

Nebuchadnezzar leads the way, his grey overcoat flapping behind him, swirling mist trailing in his wake. The natural ceiling hangs low over my head. I worry about hitting Aiden on some of the lower juts of rock. While there are no stalactites or stalagmites, azure veins tear through the stone, lighting up the crystalline structures embedded in the cave walls.

El Cid and Q trail behind us, running on the balls of their feet, swords held at the ready.

For my part, I keep the Old Lady clutched to my chest.

Red fireballs form in the chamber ahead.

Jesus, they've cut us off.

Only now do I realize they are the reason El Cid said we couldn't stop. Nebuchadnezzar and I barrel forward. He thrusts at a dyitzu with his broken pole. It ducks, but Neb just runs on by. I take a whack at it with the butt of the Old Lady and slip behind it, it's half-conscious body acting as a shield from the fire of the second dyitzu.

I look back as I race out of the room. El Cid and Q, dodging a set of fireballs, strike at the dyitzu, each slash sending lines of blood across the room.

I trip over a rock and fall, throwing my arms up in front of my face. Aiden grunts as I land, and I feel his carrier shift to the right with his weight. My arms shake as I try to push myself up. I get my torso just high enough to post one of my legs.

Blue flashing lights touch my eyes.

The Erebus.

To my left, a tunnel runs about fifty feet before opening up to a section of the most alien hellscape I've ever seen. A rushing wall of tainted black air passes over that cave opening. Streaking blue threads of slow lightning stream through the dark colored air, illuminating us and the cave with their intensity. And then the lightning is gone, and the tunnel leads only to darkness.

A hand jams itself into my armpit.

"Move!" El Cid screams. "God dammit."

Her strength and will force me to my feet. She drags me away from the cave, away from the river of darkness.

Aiden feels like he weighs a thousand pounds.

Fire whips by my head and splatters across the wall in front of me. I don't dare turn back, but the purple light of Q's sword flickers across the rocks, so I know he's protecting me.

Fuck guardian angels. I'll take an infidel any day.

"Move!" El Cid's voice cuts through my fatigue.

My feet obey her. I see Neb ahead, looking back at me, illuminated by the quick flashes of blue light coming down the corridor.

"We're almost there!" His eyes are wide, an insane grin across his face.

I'm pretty sure I can't follow him anymore.

"Aiden," I shout after the necromancer as I stumble on. "I can't . . . carry."

Nebuchadnezzar won't slow down. I turn a corner, and though I can't see the Nazi's overcoat, I see the path he'd cut into the mist. I follow.

If I can just catch up with him, I can make him carry Aiden. He has to. My legs are about as weak as my arms. I have nearly no control over my forward momentum. I trip and run into a wall, but the pain means nothing. There is no choice but to keep going.

The purple and white colored lights of their swords are close behind me again. I have to go faster. I have to.

But I don't think I can.

Then I turn a corner and run into Nebuchadnezzar nearly forcing him into the largest canyon I've ever seen.

They were right to call the Erebus a river, but it is no waterway. The air ahead of me is thick with some black, smoke-like substance—only it doesn't rise through the air like smoke does. Rather, it flows. It ripples in places and makes waves in others. The smoke is thinnest near us. I look below the precipice on which we stand and the cliff races downward, straight downward, into the abyss below. When I look up, it's the same. Infinite depths and infinite heights.

Chains of slow lightning weave their way through the flow of the river of darkness. Their brightness cuts through the opacity of the river, making small pockets of visibility and coloring them with the blue of the unchecked electricity. The lightning bolts waver back and forth in front of me, wider than the trees of Dendra, and long enough so that I cannot see their beginnings or endings. They intersect with each other, forming a tremendous tapestry of energy. Loose strands of that energy occasionally brush against the rocks of the cavern sending showers of blue sparks down like tiny rainstorms.

Neb points down. "Soulfall!" He shouts.

The man looks mad.

I look to where he's pointing and see it, an island rising out of the depths of the river.

It's an island of two peaks. The first, closest to us, is below. It looks like there was once a city built into the labyrinth of that first mountain. In places, worked stone creeps along its surface, and broken marble pillars point at where ceilings must have been. In other places, erosion or chance lightning strikes had torn away the worked rock altogether, leaving only a stone so dark it almost looks like obsidian.

As a curtain of lightning passes, I can see the valley beyond this first peak. It's a wasteland of rubble and toppled buildings. The second peak rises beyond that, cutting up through the flow of darkness and the sheets of lightning, rising higher than even where we stand. I know not what is atop it because its distance is too great, and I cannot see through the black current.

"The river!" Nebuchadnezzar shouts over the rush of the Erebus and the periodic booms created by the lightning streams as they touch down on the rock walls. "It has carved out this space here! The city was built of whetstone, which repels the electricity. That's what made Soulfall."

I collapse to my knees.

Nebuchadnezzar unstraps Aiden. The boy manages to keep his feet, which is more than I can do.

"We've got to go back!" Nebuchadnezzar's voice is as mad as his eyes.

I look along the cliff wall and see what has alarmed him. The dyitzu are leaning out from the caves which pockmark the cliffs. There is a curve in the Erebus ahead, and that gives them a direct line of fire to us.

"Forward!" El Cid yells.

She bursts around the corner, Q in tow. Q doesn't stop, but increases speed. He plants one foot on the edge of the precipice and leaps out into the abyss. His body falls down into the river, just barely missing a cord of lightning. He lands on some of Soulfall's natural rock. El Cid picks up Aiden, and then, with a couple of steps, launches him with all her body weight out into the river.

"No!" I shout.

Dyitzu fire cuts through the river's darkness. Q ducks low under one missile before standing tall and catching Aiden.

El Cid shakes her head. "It's safe!" .

Neb, eyes wide with ecstasy, leaps.

I'm incredulous, but the dyitzu are on us. El Cid slashes one's throat open.

"Jump!" she insists, "for fuck's sake!"

She opens a gash on another's torso, her white blade parting its dark skin to reveal blood and pink muscle beneath. Her next thrust slices across a dyitzu's outstretched arm, cutting into the flesh of its bicep. The muscle, perhaps cut loose from its tendon, springs back under its skin and bunches up near its shoulder.

I can hear the clicking claws of more dyitzu echoing in from the chamber beyond. I turn and jump into the Erebus.

Chapter 20

I land amidst the rubble of a ruined temple whose broken marble walls cling to the side of Soulfall.

Safe? The fuck? No. Cid lied to me.

Cid never lies, but then I realize why. Here, in the Erebus, reality bends to match our minds, to match our subconscious expectations. Here lying can be the same as telling the truth.

I look up through the debris and along the steep slope to see Q and my son picking their way forward amongst the broken stones. El Cid lands, and rolls to one side. Dyitzu fire touches down behind her, splattering across the rocks.

"To Q!" she yells. "Climb to Q."

I look back to the cliffs behind us. There are hundreds, perhaps thousands, of tiny caves which open up to the Erebus. The dyitzu are filling them up. A wave of their fire comes at us.

I am beyond tired, and I can't seem to keep enough breath in my lungs. The black air of the Erebus causes me to wheeze and cough, but I struggle forward and duck behind a pillar. Then I dare a backward glance. The thousand tiny burning orbs of dyitzu fire make a wall, a tsunami, as they approach us. A slow bolt of lightning flows through the wave, bursting some of the missiles, lighting up the sky with the rain of liquid fire—but that hardly makes a dent.

I cower behind a pillar as the wave sweeps across the side of Soulfall.

At first, it's just one dyitzu which follows us, leaping down from the cliff and landing with a thud far below. Then come its brothers. I see one get caught up in a chord, its body exploding into a burst of blood as the white-blue energy tears it apart. The rest are landing amidst the ruins.

"Too many!" Q shouts. "We have to go in!"

He stands up amidst the chest high series of dyitzu fires that surround him and points to a dark tunnel, one of the many which lead into Soulfall. I charge at it, heedless of the second barrage the dyitzu must even now be hurling at us.

I don't stop until I enter the cave. Q is there waiting for me, Aiden in his arms. Nebuchadnezzar and El Cid come in after me. I can hear the tiny rumbles of the fireballs as they strike the stones outside. Red light pours in from the cave mouth behind us.

"The passages might have collapsed deeper in," El Cid says.

"No chance out there," Q yells. "And no time.

They're coming!"

El Cid shakes her head, her lips curling into a sneer. "Come on then, after me."

We follow her into Soulfall.

It's dark. So dark that the only illumination I see is coming from the light of El Cid and Q's swords. I hear the clawed footsteps of the dyitzu behind us, following us through the tangled mess of halls and collapsed corridors. I'd give anything for one of those azure lightrock veins about now, just so we could see.

The next room has that at least, a perfect azure vein, running across the low arch of the ceiling. That might be the only lucky break we've had. The stones here have been worked over by human hands, but they must have had a cruel aesthetic. The corner stones are shaped just enough like skulls, with pits and pebbles for a toothy smile, to set me on edge. It's as if they had somehow managed to make the room oppressive—and alive, those boney heads willing the walls to close in on us.

It could only be worse if we ran into one of those ruby veins. Then the walls would look like blood.

Aiden is walking on his own. That's something good. For a moment, he turns and looks at me. I try to see some hint of blue in his eyes. He's in pain, severe pain, but it's hard to judge how far gone he is in the azure light the vein provides us with. Even so, I think I can see the hint of his iris. That's something.

"Soon," he says, his voice shaking.

Red light interrupts the soothing glow of the next room. A dyitzu has come in from behind us. I fall to the ground, the fireball sails over my head. Nebuchadnezzar decks the thing with his pole. I fight my way to my feet—reaching out to my fallen son—but Q is there, stabbing his thin purple sword through the thing's black eyeball.

Q hefts Aiden back to his feet. "Faster!"

The hallways become a blur as we run through them. El Cid seems to know which way she's going. Or maybe she doesn't, maybe we have to keep going forward because the devils are right behind us.

As if to match my previous fear, ruby veins are now running through these rooms, bathing us in their blood-colored light.

"Can you feel it?" Nebuchadnezzar asks Aiden. "Can you feel your soul?"

Aiden stops and closes his eyes for a moment.

"Move!" El Cid shouts back at us.

Aiden shakes his head. "No," his voice is faint.

I grab his hand, tugging him along.

"Stay near the back, Q." Cid orders.

"You're lost," Q accuses, "you need my help."

"They need you," she shouts back.

Why are they shouting?

Because the hellsong is so loud. Because all I can

hear is Myla's sick, low, and sultry voice humming the saddest song I've ever heard.

Q drops behind us as I drag Aiden after El Cid. None of these rooms have any natural stone at all. They are opening up though, each one sporting many more exits and hallways—a hundred new ways for the dyitzu to come at us. The ceilings are rising too. I'm hoping this gives El Cid enough options to lead us to where we need to go.

I'm guessing we're headed toward the second peak. The deeper in we travel, the more subjective reality becomes. The more subjective it is, the more likely Aiden is to be able to find his soul.

"I've seen this room before!" Nebuchadnezzar yells. "I was just thinking about it."

"We haven't gone in a circle," El Cid insists.

"Keep moving!" I shout.

The dyitzu must be close because I can hear them over the hellsong. Damn. I wonder how many followed us in here. A thousand?

"No," Nebuchadnezzar answers, his crazy blue eyes looking all around. "I mean I saw this room before, back near the Pole."

Oh shit. And the azure lighting, and the red lighting . . . I had thought of those before they happened too.

"The rooms, Cid!" Q yells from behind me. "They're taking on the nature of our thoughts."

El Cid shakes her head. "But there are no Furies! We can't be that far in yet."

"It's happening, Cid!" Q shouts.

She leads us deeper in. I can practically hear the dyitzu breathing behind us.

El Cid seems more confident now, leading us quickly from room to room with a purpose.

"The shape of the rooms are the same!" she shouts. "It's just the features we're adding."

She must have taken us in a circle, maybe to test her theory, because we come upon a pair of surprised dyitzu from behind. They turn at the sound of her voice and hurl fire. She cuts them down with wide, quick strokes.

"That may not keep happening as we go deeper in," Nebuchadnezzar says. "The stone of the rooms themselves might change."

Aiden stops, putting his hands on his knees. I'd pick him up if I could, but the most I can do is grab his hand and drag him with us.

"Pay attention to the rooms," Cid says. "We'll have to remember them to get back."

Oh you've got to be kidding me. I'm barely awake enough to think, let alone memorize the rooms we're running through. I do my best to remember them by their shape and by the color of the crystals or the vein of lightrock, but when I try to recall them, they've fled from my mind. Maybe I can just remember a little, and someone else can remember a different part. Together we might find our way back.

The rooms become hypnotic, as if each one is a single note in a vile lullaby, tricking my mind into relaxing. And it needs to relax so badly. My body is dying, my lungs are aching, and the muscles in my arms are so full of blood I can barely move them. Aiden stumbles on behind me, my reason for existence.

I see a shadow of a man down a side corridor. He darts away.

No one else seems to have seen him.

"There are people down here!" I warn.

"You're seeing things," Q yells back.

"I saw someone." Unless I'm insane. Unless that was a figment of my mad mind impressing itself upon the world around us.

"You must have seen a dyitzu," El Cid shouts.

"I know what I saw!"

They don't believe me. Cid's leading us up a series of long corridors now, but I think we're still heading in a straight line away from where we entered. I think. There's no way to know.

"Shit!" Q yells.

Aiden is trying to stop again. I grab his wrist more forcefully. He turns his head and vomits. My heart dies in my chest. His body is half dead, his organs half turned, and we're taking him at a full run through this hell.

"What?" El Cid calls back.

"Cris is right, we are not alone."

"Your minds are making it up," she says.

"I don't think so, Cid."

"But this place has been abandoned since . . . I mean, it hasn't been safe to come here for two thousand years."

But I feel what Q is feeling. There's something below us, far below us maybe, but I sense its evil, its dark intentions, radiating up through Soulfall, this world which is changing to match its malice.

Myla's voice is joyous. It rises from the lowest depths of despair to the highest notes of ecstasy. But joy isn't the right word. I can feel the music in my bones. It overpowers all that I can hear.

Aiden must feel better after his vomiting because the hellsong is coming from his mind—or at least, that's what I think. We've all heard her voice, now.

We run down a long hallway. Just as we leave it, I see dyitzu pouring in.

"Behind!" Q warns.

El Cid takes us along a quick series of turns and then down a set of stairs. The dyitzu might have been able to keep up, but with the hellsong so loud, I doubt they can hear our footsteps.

Christ, I'm lost. We're not going to be able to find our way out of here again. This labyrinth will be our tomb.

Apparently satisfied that we lost them, El Cid slows and leads us into the next room.

There is a man there, dressed in dyitzu skin leathers, barefoot and unarmed.

"Salvete," he says, his voice hollow.

"Salve," El Cid answers, walking by him.

We follow her, and the man starts to follow us. Hell. Is he an enemy? Will he attack? What language was he speaking?

He shouts some more words.

"What's he saying?" Q asks.

"Babbling," El Cid says. "I think he's insane."

And the rooms seem to match his state of mind. They have become twisted and odd. Stairways lead up into walls. Doors jut out from ceilings. El Cid takes us through a hallway that dead ends. She turns around.

"I'm lost!" Q shouts.

"Me too," El Cid answers.

My blood runs cold, but she keeps us moving. She's got to. Lost or no, the dyitzu are still behind us.

The next room has stone ribs coming out of the walls. The top half of a human is trapped there. The ribs press across his body, keeping him still against the grey stone. The ruby red light covers him over, and his guts, strung out from his torso, form a small pile on the ground where they glisten in the light. This man speaks as well, perhaps in that same language. Cid ignores him.

"We're going down!" Q yells. "We need to go up."

El Cid turns, the red light masking the green of her eyes. "There's no way up."

So we go down.

I hear something over the hellsong. A raven calling perhaps? Or several of them. We come into the next room. It too has the rib cage walls, but its floor is covered with tiny grey-skinned babies. There are toddlers in the back, eating some of the younger ones. Then I realize the babies are trying to eat each other as well, gnawing their siblings' limbs with their toothless gums. In the back of the room, held down by the stone ribs in the wall, is a pregnant woman. She's screaming, though I can barely hear her over the hellsong. Even as she shouts an infant comes head first out of her distended vagina. It drops to the ground, its placenta following. The smell of fetid and perverse afterbirth assaults me.

One of the older children picks up the gooey organic mass and starts to eat it. Another chews at the umbilical cord, slurping it up into its mouth like it was some giant piece of spaghetti. The freshly born infant reaches out with one of his skinny arms and grabs hold of one of its brothers. It tries to eat the ankle with a strength and dexterity which should be beyond a newborn—only without teeth, not much happens. The real damage is done on the right side of the room where the children are older.

They are fighting and wrestling, rolling amidst the younger infants, crushing them, sometimes devouring them. They get older as I follow them around the circle of this room until I make it back to the woman. There, one of those grey skinned children has grown old enough to become an adolescent. He's aroused.

He enters his mother, but pulls away quickly as another child comes out.

The mother screeches.

I feel something pressing against the shoes Jessica gave me. One of the babies is trying to eat through the leather.

"We have to go forward!" Q yells over the hellsong and the sound of a thousand crying, dying and feeding children.

"We'll hurt them!" El Cid yells.

A toddler has made it over to Nebuchadnezzar. "You killed us!" Its tiny voice holds a strange and special hatred. "You killed our mothers. You killed our fathers."

Not good.

The mass of children starts moving toward us. Even the infants, who should be too young to understand or even crawl. Hell, maybe none of them should even speak English.

Q grabs Cid by the shoulder. "Now, Cid!"

El Cid's sword flicks back and forth, tearing a way through the room. The children shout in pain. The toddlers clutch at their wounds and cower. The adolescents slink away, teeth bared. The infants cry as she crushes them beneath her boots. Q falls in behind her, his purple sword widening the path. Aiden follows that path of blood and death. I hear the sorrowful crying of the mother. She must be in so much pain, and she must be insane, but for some reason her tears sound fresh, as if the wound was new.

Maybe it would be worth it to cut our way to her and kill her—to save her from this Hell.

But El Cid doesn't take us that way. We come toward the back of the chamber. The woman's crying doesn't stop, it keeps with us. It is so soulful I want to cry myself. I cover my ears and yell. It's like before, when El Cid insulted me, and the part of my mind that was supposed to defend me from insults had failed. Only now the pain is so much worse. How long has that woman been here . . .

El Cid turns, and I realize it isn't the mother who's crying.

Tears are rolling down her face, washing away the blood of the children she'd just murdered. Snot pours freely from her nose. She's shaking violently with her grief.

I wonder what it must have been like for her to cut through those grey children. I wonder, had she been anything other than an infidel, if she would have even been able to do it.

I fall to my knees in front of her and wrap her up in a hug. From behind us, the sounds of dyitzu fire and shouting babies echo in. El Cid sobs in my arms like Aiden might. I'd forgotten how small she is. The tears and snot soak into my shirt.

She shakes and shakes and shakes.

The children, she must have somehow managed to love every single one of them.

Q grabs her shoulder with one hand. "Come on!" I hear him shout. "Come on! They're coming."

But El Cid can't move. She's stayed strong this whole time, while the rest of us broke down. We acted on our hearts and made her do the hard work. We made her override us when we were too irrational. We made her come up with the solutions when we had none.

"Now!" Q screams.

He pulls us both to our feet and pushes us along. Aiden is ahead of us and Neb is trying to catch up.

"Do you know where we are?" Q is yelling at El Cid.

She's still crying, and she's not even focused on him. A dyitzu rounds the corner. I hit it in the face with the Old Lady.

It drops to the ground, its clawed fingers clutching at its eyes. I ram the butt of my shotgun into its skull again and again.

I turn back to Q and Cid.

"Do you know?" Q is shouting at her. "Which

direction to the upper mountain?"

El Cid is focusing on him now, but her eyes are still full of sorrow. "I don't know."

For the first time in my life, I see what Q's face looks like when he's afraid.

Chapter 21

El Cid falls back against a stone wall. Q's nervous eyes are glancing all around us. Neb's mask is long gone. He's brushing his hands over his grey trenchcoat, again and again and again and again. Aiden sits down and looks back toward the room with the children. Some were his own age. Some of the ones we killed, even.

Myla's voice is as clear as a bell. It rings softly through the halls, reminding me of futures we could have had. Of the things we missed in the Old World. Of what it might have been like to grow old with each other. It was Hell that tore us apart. On Earth, things would have been different. I can see her now, standing at my grave. She's old. Sad. Crying.

She lays orchids on the ground where my body would have rested.

It's like that, you know, for a person who spent fifty years loving another. Fucking and kissing and hating and fighting and holding and singing. I can't think of such things, I have to think of the shape of the rooms. El Cid said that the rock didn't change, only what was imprinted on the rock did. But how could she know? If, in such a place, believing a thing made it true, how could she know whether the underlying rock really was the same, or if it was her expectation that made it seem so?

The brained dyitzu's blood is creeping across the floor. One thing is certain, we can't stay here.

"Follow me!" I shout.

El Cid struggles back to her feet. Q moves to pick up Aiden, but my boy waves him off.

"I can run," Aiden says. "The pain, it isn't bad here."

"Can you feel it yet?" Neb's voice is thick with a German accent. "Can you feel the ether?"

Aiden shakes his head.

I plow forward into the dark.

I hear their footsteps behind me. There must be some way to figure this maze out. There has to be a way we can get across to the far mountain. But how can I begin to find out where I'm going if I don't know if El Cid was right when she said the stone can't move?

There is a way to know. We could have other people, who didn't know or believe that stricture, walk into those rooms and measure them. Then we could compare their measurements with hers.

Damn, now I get it.

I realize why there's no magic. Because even when magic is real, the only way to understand it is to understand its nature. The entire idea of the supernatural is bullshit. Even here, surrounded by a supernatural reality, surrounded by relativism, the only way to make any progress in understanding is to think analytically about it. The stuff of the Erebus, the ether of the world Nebuchadnezzar just mentioned, it exists — and anything that exists must do so under a set of circumstances. It must have nature.

That's what Q meant about Earth's lightning being magic. It was pretty awesome, an unmeasurable energy that strikes backward, whose parts, electrons, could be in two places at once, and could ignore causality. What could be more supernatural than that? But lightning is completely natural. Humans had missed the boat! We kept looking around us for magic and magicians, but we had missed the fact that we had already learned the magic and become the magicians ourselves.

So it doesn't really matter if I know the way up to the second mountain. What matters is that the most powerful subconscious around us *believes* I know the way—and if the hellsong is any indication—that subconscious is Aiden's.

"Where are we?" Nebuchadnezzar shouts.

"Getting close!" I yell back.

Q's face is blank.

El Cid is right behind him. She's got a crooked little grin behind her tears.

Nebuchadnezzar is just behind Aiden, his pole

swinging back and forth as he runs. "The hell do you think you're taking us?"

I stop, turn and grab him by the shoulders. "I know the way! I figured it out."

For a moment he doesn't believe me, but then his skepticism breaks. Maybe he can see the grin I feel on my face. Maybe it doesn't look as mad as I think it must. Maybe his wish-thinking is getting the better of him again. Hell, it could even be that he figured out how believing in me might be self-fulfilling—but whatever the case—the key is that Aiden saw him believe in me. And as long as Aiden buys this, we're home free.

Myla's music sounds a little less sad.

My friends and son, they eagerly follow me now as I race onward, downward, into the depths. When I round the next corner, I see a bundle of orchids. They're the ones I imagined just moment's ago. I hear Myla's singing, but it's different now. She's singing a song I know. A song that was my lullaby when I was dying of cancer.

In a cavern, in a canyon,
Excavating for a mine,
Lived a miner, forty-niner
And his daughter Clementine.

The dyitzu come at us while Myla sings us the chorus. One of their clawed feet crushes the heads of some of the orchids. El Cid's white blade snakes out into the darkness as Neb and I rush forward. I duck below a fireball and end up tripping to the ground, but Neb keeps going. He's swinging away at them as I regain my feet. They're not all dead, but we keep running.

I can see the other people, now, the hopeless souls down here. They've been lost so long, their minds feeding into the environment, the environment feeding into their minds. They must be mad.

Light she was and like a fairy, Myla sings on.

And her shoes were number nine

Herring boxes without topses

Sandals weren't for Clementine.

The Erebus, it's fighting against me. I tried to be optimistic, I tried to convince them I knew which way to go, but I feel its hopelessness creeping in around the edges. I can see the dead look in Aiden's all-but-black eyes.

But he's running. He's awake. He's as alive now as he's been in weeks. I will not let this place take me because dying here is only the second worst thing that can happen.

Drove she ducklings to the water

Every morning just at nine,

Hit her foot against a splinter

Fell into the foaming brine.

More stone ribcages line the walls. I see the poor bastards who've been trapped here for only the Devil knows how long, caught up behind the granite cage bars. If we fail, we'll end up like them. Not dead, no . . . the Erebus, or that hatred emanating from below us, would never let the dyitzu finish us off so quickly. This one is eviscerated, just like the man we saw before, only there are rats eating at his guts. His guts must be regrowing at just the right speed because the rats don't seem to be making any progress.

But that's nothing.

That's not pain.

I round the next corner to see my own grave.

Ruby lips above the water, Myla sings.

Blowing bubbles soft and fine,

It looks exactly like the one I'd imagined. Exactly, and I feel the weight of those fifty imagined years of grief because here, in this Hell, imagination is reality.

But alas, I was no swimmer,

So I lost my Clementine.

The hell is wrong with this song? How the fuck do I know the lyrics? It has to be someone else. It can't be coming from my mind.

"Leave it!" I yell, jumping over my own grave.

"But it's got your—" Aiden begins.

"I said leave it!"

But he doesn't know that it came from my mind. He thinks it's Hell that put the grave there.

Jesus, he might start to lose faith in me.

How I missed her! How I missed her!

How I missed my Clementine,

Till I killed her little sister,

And forgot my Clementine.

The fuck? That can't be how the song went. Hell must be warping the words or something.

Stairs, leading us up! Thank the fucking Infidel. Something is going right for us.

Then the miner, forty-niner,

Soon began to peak and pine,

I thought he oughter join his daughter,

Now he's with his Clementine.

"Shut up!" I yell. "Myla, that's not how the song goes!"

But Myla isn't here, or at least she's not really here, and shouting her name only makes the figment of her singing to us become more real.

Aiden stops, one foot poised in the air over the next step. I look with him back down the long flight of stairs. Q, Cid and Neb turn around too. There's a naked little girl at the bottom. Her skin might be grey, like the babies before, but it's hard to tell in the light. She's emaciated, and I can see her ribs and the awkward juts of her hips beneath her sunken stomach.

Neb shrieks. He stumbles backward onto the stairs, his feet kicking to try and propel him upward.

The girl's mouth opens. "Ich kann Sie nicht sehen!" Her voice is high pitched and desperate. "Ich kann Sie nicht sehen!"

Q helps Neb to his feet and I start backing up the

stairs. She's speaking German, so she's obviously from the Necromancer's mind.

"She's not real, Neb!" I yell. "You're imagining. . ."

But it doesn't matter if he imagined her or not. The fact that she came from his mind does *not* mean she's not real.

I trip over something on the stairs. It's a shoe, an old looking shoe, like one a child might wear. And there is another on the next step, and another. Some are for adults, some for children. Some for men, and some for women. They're all made in an elder style, though, like something from the 40s or 50s.

There is light above and the stairs lead us into a room—a huge room—filled with so many shoes that they form a fifty foot mountain, soaring up almost halfway to the dark ceiling.

I check back down the steps, but I don't see the girl.

I see an exit on the far side of the room ahead. I step onto the mass of footwear. It's like trudging through snow. Hell, maybe one of these pairs would be better for me than Jessica's.

Everyone is following me, step by step—except Nebuchadnezzar.

The shoes seem almost to melt away under his feet as he steps and they cling to him as he tries to climb after us. El Cid reaches back and grabs his arm. He pushes forward with her help. It's getting worse, the shoes are dragging him down. El Cid's strength isn't enough to help.

He's waist deep.

Q grabs his other arm and starts pulling. Aiden and I stop. I rush back down a few steps, bringing a small avalanche of shoes with me.

Shoulder deep.

Neb looks horrified. This must be a room from his mind, but what could it possibly mean? How could something as innocuous as shoes hold such terror in his psyche?

"Come on, Neb!" I shout. "We need you for the Furies!"

Neck deep. Q and El Cid are pulling, but his weight is taking them down.

El Cid is shouting at Neb, but I can't hear her over the hellsong. God, how many shoes did he imagine? A million? Two?

Fear takes me.

Six.

Six million pairs of shoes. I'd learned that in school. At the camps they'd take the victims' belongings and sort them into tremendous piles.

"We forgive you!" El Cid is shouting.

The hellsong is all wrong. It's not Myla anymore. It's a girl calling, in German, "Ich kann Sie nicht sehen!"

"*I said we forgive you!*" El Cid's voice cracks as she screams.

Neb looks up at her, blue eyes wide. For a moment

he stops sinking.

"We forgive you," she continues. "You're not one of them anymore, Neb. You're a traitor. You betrayed them. It took you a long time, but it happened. You're on our side now. Do you understand? On *our* side."

Nebuchadnezzar is crying. All his pretentions of mental health and stability are lost. In their place is the pathetic shell of a war criminal who's suddenly been forced to come face to face with his own mind.

Soulfall has given his conscience teeth.

"They'll never forgive me," he insists.

"We do!" El Cid spits as she yells. "I speak for us. I forgive you. We forgive you. You're fighting with us—"

"The Infidel," I interrupt. "Say it now. Accept his offer. He can absolve you of your guilt. You know he can. He wouldn't have offered it to you if he couldn't."

Those Aryan eyes open with wonder, and for a moment, it seems as if he truly can be redeemed.

"Ich nehme an," he whispers. "Nehme an."

He crawls forward, and the shoes seem to no longer want him. Symbolically, it's a Jewish girl and a black man who drag him to his feet.

We make our way around the mountain as fast as we can manage before climbing into the passageway beyond.

There the Infidel, or the figment of him, sits waiting for us.

"He loves you," the Infidel tells Aiden.

Then he nods back over his shoulder to where more stairs rise. At the top of those stairs I see the swirling darkness of the Erebus. The hellsong mounts in my ears, but I don't give a damn about its version of Clementine.

We're getting Aiden as close to Sheol as we can, and I'll kill anything real or dreamed that stands in my way. Q and Cid rush past me as I drag the gaping Aiden away from the Infidel.

Chapter 22

I hear it now, a distant noise, a shout or a call or something like that. It reminds me of a train.

"The Furies." El Cid freezes where she is on the top stair. "It's time," she says quickly.

Q turns to me. He kneels, but since he's a few steps up, his eyes are level with mine. He offers me his sword, hilt first.

I take the blade.

"No," Aiden's small voice trembles. "We need you!"

"They can't help us," Nebuchadnezzar says. "Nothing can face the Furies. Nothing. I can trick them, make them attack the undead on the upper city, but no one can defeat them."

El Cid drops to one knee as well and offers her small white sword to Aiden. He takes it. The blade trembles in his tight fist, its white light vibrating across the stones. The sword, sized perfectly for El Cid, seems oddly large in his hands. El Cid hurriedly takes one step down. For a moment, I look up into her beyond-green eyes. She puts one hand behind the back of my head, cupping my neck. She pulls me forward and presses her tiny lips into mine. For half a second, her tongue flicks along my tongue.

She takes my pack and passes me by.

Q slings Neb's pack over his shoulder and embraces me fiercely. "I know you have to do this, live or die."

He follows her.

"I'll be right after you!" Neb shouts to them.

For a heartbeat, I watch the infidels descend the stairs. Without them, I feel naked. I shouldn't. I faced a decade of Hell on my own. And technically, I'm one of them. Only, without much of their training, I don't feel like an infidel.

"Follow me." My voice sounds rough, confident . . . not at all how I actually feel.

I run up into the Erebus, toward the rush of the dark air and the streamers of electricity, headlong into the nightmare reality, toward the call of the Furies and the wall of undead, toward the life of my son.

I can tell where Aiden is behind me from the bouncing glimmers of white light that reflect off the stone bricks and rubble which line the mountain ahead of us. I climb its steep slope. I turn back to look out across Soulfall. . . and I shouldn't have.

The cliff wall beyond rises like eternity. Distant now, small as ants, I can see the silhouettes of the dyitzu in their caves. Their fire starts coming at us, defiantly shining out as miniscule pin pricks of red light which grow infinitesimally larger as they approach through the torrential ripples of the Erebus.

The stuff of the river presses now against my skin, like an unholy wind. I feel it rustling through my hair and soaking into my clothes. I watch it part just slightly around Q's blade. Its rush is a hollow sound in my ears. Over it, and very faintly, I hear the long cries of the Furies.

I look to my right, upstream, to watch the rush of the river and the cords of electricity. I see the score marks on the stone where the lightning had touched down some time ago. I hop up over a broken stone wall and climb along the side of a pillar. The stones are slick under my free hand and the dark taint of the Erebus collects on my fingers. I'm breathing it in. The air is bad, but so am I.

"Almost there!" Nebuchadnezzar calls.

To his right, woefully off target, a ball of dyitzu fire explodes against the side of the mountain. There is no way to climb and keep watch behind me to make sure that I don't get hit by a lucky blast. All I can do is hope as I crawl up the mountain.

I spot another shortcut, a crumbling wall that had once been the side of a building. I try to climb it, and maybe I could have if I wasn't carrying Q's sword. Instead, I give up halfway, and run laterally across the ruins of Soulfall until I see a set of wide marble steps.

A dyitzu fireball explodes in front of me, its red light welcome in the sea of dimness that surrounds me. I step around it as I hurry up the steps to the plateau.

There are the dead.

It's not really a plateau at all, but an agora made of obsidian-black whetstone bricks. Nothing can cut whetstone, except apparently for the stonemasons of the Ancients. Perhaps that substance repels the lightning like Neb was saying, but over the centuries, the streams of electricity appear to have leveled many of the buildings whose ruins surround this black-bricked plain.

My legs are burning in pain, but there is no time. I run forward as fast as I can.

The undead are spread evenly throughout the agora. The closest ones notice us. They turn their heads first, and then their bodies. As they do so, they disturb the ones behind them.

I skid to a halt.

In places beyond the mass of the dead, along the edge of the plateau, black pillars of forgotten buildings still stand like the blackened bones of long dead skeletons.

The dead start advancing, a few at a time.

Now I see the far wall—I see Sheol. There, across from us is the Hell beyond, my next afterlife, my next destiny. The place that I have to take Aiden to the edge of, if only to ensure he does not go there.

But there is no way to get Aiden close to it. The corpses are too thick. Even if we still had bullets, even if we had Q and El Cid, I'm not sure we could fight our way through them. All this way to fail? Maybe we can climb around the edges. Get on the cliff and . . . but that's too slow. The Furies are coming.

Hell, the dead are coming.

Maybe we're close enough.

"Can you feel it?" I shout to my son. "The ether?"

He closes his eyes and extends his fingers. Then his head shakes. "No."

Neb puts a hand on my right shoulder. "There!" He shouts, pointing ahead.

His grey overcoat, stained with the blood of children and the black soot-like residue of the Erebus, ripples in the wind-like current.

"What?" I shout.

"There! The bridge! We need to get Aiden there."

I see what he's pointing at, on the far side of the agora, but there's too many of the dead.

"The corpses!" I shout.

The first of them is only ten feet away. I dart forward on shaky legs and swing Q's sword. I miss, my blade coming up short, but I get the thing across the jaw with my backswing and again in the chest as it stumbles forward. Q's blade is unbelievably light and preternaturally sharp. The corpse falls to my feet.

"Stand back!" Neb shouts.

Another is going for Aiden. I take a couple of side steps and stab it in the ribs. It turns, clawing at me. One of its soot-covered hands grabs my shirt and I feel its rotten nails cutting into my flesh. The Furies howl with my anguish. I turn Q's blade and kick the corpse back. There's more, many more, some only twenty feet away, standing shoulder to shoulder. There's no way I can cut that many down. We've got to run, only I can't make myself do that. I've come too far. I'm too tired. It's time to die.

El Cid will understand.

I breathe in the dark air and scream.

"I said stand back!" Neb's voice cuts through the howl of the wind and the Furies. "*Zurücktreten!*"

I do as he says. Aiden steps up next to me.

The grey Nazi overcoat falls off of Neb's shoulders. He walks forward to meet the wall of undead. They are wearing the clothes of the ancients, white togas turned black in the centuries they'd been exposed to the Erebus. Who knows what lives they lived before equal parts of Hell and corpsedust twisted them to serve this dark purpose.

Neb holds his hand to the sky and the rush of the Erebus obeys his command—and of course it does, because here, in Soulfall, the world around us obeys our minds. The bad air rushes around him, half whirlpool, half dust devil, roiling and spinning. His blond hair and dark undershirt whip about in the wind. Hair and flakes of dead skin come off of the corpses, swirling about in the gusts.

He holds forth his pouch, filled with the products of whatever mad alchemy he has at his disposal. Of course he doesn't fear the dead. He is their master, their piper, their king—their Fuehrer.

He digs a handful of dust out and holds it over his head, offering it to the Erebus. The current picks it up, swirling it around to the drumbeat of hellsong, spreading it in concentric circles across the mass of undead, across me and my son, across the shells of buildings.

The undead stop, and they turn away.

That's when I see the Furies.

Neb is shouting in my ear and grabbing at my shirt. I can feel the cloth brushing against the wounds the corpse left in my shoulder, but I don't care.

I see *them*.

Three Furies, swimming upstream through the Erebus. Distant white lights, like angels, darting toward us. They look like women, white robes flying behind them. They are too far away for me to be sure, but I think they have many arms.

"... too random..." Neb's voice sound's hoarse. "I couldn't get . . ." The three Furies call together, and I cannot hear the necromancer over them. ". . . do you understand? I couldn't get them all . . . some will still attack you."

A dyitzu fireball crests the stairs behind us, soaring up through the endless abyss.

I try to focus on Nebuchadnezzar. The undead. He didn't get all the undead. Some will still attack us.

"You have to . . . now!" He's shaking me. "Now, Cris! You . . . to take Aiden now!"

Nebuchadnezzar turns and runs.

I hold out my left hand. Aiden doesn't seem to be in any pain. And why would he? Nebuchadnezzar told him the Erebus would take away his misery, and so it has. I feel his small hand in mine. I see the ones Neb was talking about, the undead he didn't affect. They are coming toward us still, but they are adrift in the sea of Neb's mob.

Aiden and I move through the crowd, darting with them and around them. The hands of our enemies come at us from behind the shoulders of dead strangers. I cut at the dead, ducking beneath their reaching arms. I do my best to keep Aiden clear of them, but mostly we just run. We knock good and evil corpses away with equal vigor. The drumbeat of the hellsong is loud enough to shake my heart, and it grows stronger as we approach the bridge. Of course it would, our minds gain strength over the environment as we make our progress.

Aiden gives out a small shout. One corpse has managed to grab hold of his shoulder. He stabs up at it with El Cid's white blade. The thing jerks back, dead hands clutching, ripping off a piece of Aiden's ear. I strike at it too and drag my son around another corpse. The slick motor oil of a half man, half wight leaks down the side of his neck.

The next one catches my thigh. I hack at the limb, once, twice, three times, before I disengage it, ripping off some of my pants and some of my skin with the effort.

The first of the Furies comes, traveling through the stone pillars at the edge of the agora as if they weren't even there. She tilts back her head and howls into the rush of the Erebus. I hear nothing but her. I still feel the drumbeat of the hellsong in the hollow of my chest, but its sound is lost in the vehemence of the cry. Her eight arms draw eight blades, and she sets about herself, striking at the corpses. She floats through them, a swath of death. The bodies of the corpses, sometimes torn apart from the force of her blows, spread around her in all directions.

I have never seen such power.

Another corpse tries to grab me. I duck and run my shoulder into it, sending it back into the crowd. Aiden cuts at a good undead and a bad one, sending coagulated chunks of corpseblood into the air.

One hundred yards.

This far out, it seems there are more of the corpses Nebuchadnezzar didn't touch, or maybe they've just had more time to gather around us. We hack indiscriminately as we rush forward. One rips open the bottom of my pant leg, drawing a long bloody cut down my calf. I try to interpose a good corpse between us, but that one turns on me and strikes.

Its fingernails scratch long lines across my chest.

I run my sword through its face and use its convulsing body to block the path of the one behind me.

Seventy-five yards.

Another Fury comes to the agora, adding its own deafening cry to the fray. The third will be here soon. A corpse, once a woman, bites into my arm, the one I'm using to hold Aiden's hand. I lose his grip. I bring the hilt down on the back of her neck and stab out into the face of the next corpse. I have no idea if it was turned by Neb's dust or not. Aiden's fighting now too, his white blade picking up speed. It's as if he was born to do this.

Fifty yards.

He is light on his feet.

Of course he is, the Erebus gives us energy, didn't you know? I breathe it in and feel its dark ether spreading throughout my limbs. It gives me strength like nothing else can. Except I don't even need it. Here, my mind alone can move my body.

Maybe it can move corpses too. Here, corpse, do my bidding, move.

Maybe it's moved by my mind, or maybe it's just one of the corpses Neb's powder had hit, I'm not sure—

but it steps aside.

Twenty-five yards.

The third Fury is here, killing and screaming its way toward the other two, but I don't care. Its horrid voice is no longer enough to overpower the hellsong which is singing to me—not with Myla's voice, but with the song of angels, of demons, of humans and Nazis, all crying for one thing. They want me to make it to the bridge.

Suddenly we're between the ruins of buildings. The bridge is unearthly, a twenty foot wide structure that heads out into the rushing current of the dark air. It's made of the same black whetstone as the bricked surface of the agora. On either side of the bridge are two stone guard rails, each about three feet tall. But the bridge ends, abruptly, as if the lightning tore it apart.

Aiden runs up to its jagged edge and stops. I follow and turn my back to him. Three corpses are coming at me. I hack at them, sending one flailing over the edge. The second one falls under my blows, and the last I beat down with the hilt, its ancient skull crumpling beneath the infidel-forged metal.

Aiden stands, one hand held before him. "I feel it!" His voice is tiny, and all but drowned out by the hellsong and the wind and the Furies, but he shouts it again. "I feel it!"

He can touch his own soul.

Another corpse stumbles onto the bridge. At this

point, I don't care. Let a Fury come. It ain't getting by me.

I slice it across the face once, twice, three times. It goes down by the bodies of the others. I turn back and see them, five more Furies, coming across the abyss from Sheol. They're only tiny white spots, but I know how fast those things move. I hope we have time.

I step up to the precipice by my son and ready Q's sword.

Then it happens.

The dark air around my son shimmers. A white light shines down through the darkness to cover his shoulders. He stands there, colorless, illuminated in greys and blacks and whites. The energy pulses down around him. It rolls over and through him. The air about him starts to rise, rushing upward from the abyss below. His hair flutters and his shirt billows with the sudden updraft. As if drawn up by the wind, his arms rise.

I don't care if we make it back through this Hell or not. That's not what's important. What matters is that for this one moment, this one God damned moment, I have my son back. I don't deserve this, and maybe no man does. I wasn't a good father. There were times when I yelled at him, when I hit him, when I disciplined him too much, when I crushed his soul in the way that only a father can . . . but I'm only human. I didn't do my best, but I did what I could. I tried hard, and I've spent the last three years pouring my heart out into the search for him, into his rescue, into his salvation from this dark disease his mother afflicted him with.

I look behind me now as my son glows with the healing power of his own mind, look through the skeletons of buildings and the mob of corpses and the streaks of death left by the howling furies. Look to the downslope of this mountain to the tiny balls of fire which still rain in from the dyitzu beyond. I know that between us and the Hell I knew is the maze of dark caverns and nightmare that we traversed to get here.

It's clear to me now that we won't make it back. It's clear to me now that this is where I die.

But that's okay.

Sometimes you have to let things go.

All I want is my son back.

The wind slows and the light dims and Aiden's clothes settle. His face is tilted upward, eyes closed. The last of the glow leaves his pale cheeks. His is a face of contentment. Of bliss. Of health after being so sick for so long.

He opens his eyes.

His black eyes.

His pitch black eyes.

Suddenly I can't see him well through the tears. I stumble backward, falling over a corpse. Q's sword clatters against the stones as I hit the guard rail. Bits of ancient rock break away and tumble into the abyss behind me.

"But . . ."

Why? Didn't he love me? I thought that he wouldn't die without my permission. I can practically hear his voice saying the words . . .

I pick up my sword and stand.

He wouldn't die without his father's permission — and I was arrogant enough to think that he meant me. He was talking about the Archdevil. He was talking about Myla's other lover. Aiden was so young when she took him, he probably barely remembered me. Was I really this arrogant? Had I really thought he would see me as his father after such a short time? All he'd seen me do was kill his new, nearly all-powerful dad — and murder his mother. He didn't love me. He loved that demon. That thing.

And now he has become what his adopted father always wanted. He is a wight.

No wonder he'd only stayed on edge when we kept him sedated. When he was awake, he was fighting, not to live, but to die.

The smile on his face is the most evil, the must gut-wrenching, the most hope crushing thing I've ever seen.

Q told me once that I should abandon him and have a new child, and maybe there was wisdom in that.

The smile on Aiden's face disappears. In its place is a kind of pure rage that only a young man can have. *"You killed her!"* His voice no longer has trouble cutting through the cacophony.

This is his moment. His father killed his mother, and now he's getting his revenge. He must know the pain that is tearing through my soul. In that way, in his thirst for revenge, he is very much like me.

I take a deep breath of the Erebus air and let it all go. The pain. The failure. The fear. And when those things are gone, only the love I have for my son remains.

I think I've learned something about being a father. I think I've learned what it means to love a child. Father's don't get to choose what kind of men their sons become. They can hope, and they can coach, but in the end it's the boy's decision. He decides what kind of man he'll be. Aiden had been forced to grow up fast in the Hell he was born in. This is his decision.

It's time I let him go.

"Run." I tell him, turning to the approaching Furies. "I'll hold them off."

He's stunned. His black eyes widen as his pale face slackens.

For a second, he does nothing. "But . . ."

"I love you, son," I yell. "You have to choose who you're going to be. I can't do that for you. If you want to be a wight, then that's what you'll be. Now go, run! Don't let the infidels see you."

He's motionless. "But I'll kill the people you love."

I look at him. "Aiden, you are the people I love." I

turn to face the howling eight-armed white angels. "Now go!"

His white sword is shaking in his hands. I learn now that wights can cry.

Finally, he runs, jumping over the slain corpses, heading back toward Soulfall.

I step up to the edge of the bridge and look out into the abyss, to the oncoming rush of the five Furies, to their forty arms and forty blades. I need not kill them. I just have to give Aiden some time.

Jesus had it the wrong way round, you see. It's not the son that should be sacrificed.

"Cris!" I hear him shout. "Help me!"

I turn, glancing over my shoulder. There he is at the foot of the bridge. For a moment, as a bolt of lightning rushes by, he's just a silhouette. Behind him is the sea of undead and the ripples of the Erebus. The three Furies already on the plateau are cutting the dead down around them, sending their mangled corpses out in all directions. A series of fireballs, so far away they're barely be visible, coast along the river of darkness, soaring like distant birds over our heads, curving with the current.

The undead are flocking to Aiden. Shit. Now he's a wight. The corpses Neb turned must now view him as their enemy.

Why can't I just die?

I run to him.

Chapter 23

Unlike the dead, we know to run from the Furies. There are eight of them on Soulfall now, and I see dozens more coming from both upriver and down.

When we leave the plateau we will be horribly vulnerable as there will be no other targets.

It's easier, with the dead's number so thinned out, to run across the black brick of whetstone. I strike down one corpse that reaches at me.

We come to the steps.

Aiden is fearless. He descends the stairs and starts hopping down the mountain, from rock to rock, letting his momentum carry him on. For some reason I want to pause after each leap, to catch my balance before charging forward, but there's no time.

A single slip, and I'll die.

I see the tunnel ahead of us as we race down—and I dare a backward glance.

Two Furies leave the plateau and head toward us.

Jesus. They can travel through stone, so they'll cut through the maze of Soulfall as if it wasn't even there while Aiden and I will be forced to run around corridors and hallways.

"No time!" I shout. "We have to climb over!"

Who knows if we have any chance of getting by the dyitzu which were crawling over the mountainside when we last left it, but I'd fight them before fighting a Fury. We start ascending the lower mount, half climbing, half running. It's less steep on this side, and we make better progress.

We arrive at the summit. I look to the cliffs of Gehenna ahead of us. There are still some dyitzu there, but not nearly as many as there were before. I guess most of them are running around in that maze inside Soulfall.

I take another look behind. The Furies are closer. Maybe they know that we're the cause of all this. Maybe they couldn't sense us in this eddy of the Erebus before, but they sure as hell can now.

We skip over the rocks, charging down the mountain. I feel the Furies' calls on the back of my neck. They grow louder and louder. I shout to Aiden, but I can't even hear my own voice.

The dyitzu on the rocks ahead of us turn and flee. Even they dare not face these things.

Aiden is running faster than I thought a boy could. Maybe the mad world around us is lending its strength to his stride in accordance with his belief, or maybe his wight limbs give him more power—or maybe he's just running for his life.

There's only one problem, we're running out of Soulfall.

And there, I see them, Q and El Cid and Neb, standing on the cliff across from us. One of the Furies is focused on the dyitzu, but another is heading toward us. I know I will feel one of its blades cutting through my back. Its call is shaking my insides, vibrating my heart with its intensity. I must be deaf.

Aiden sees the infidels and stops. I hope like hell they haven't spotted him.

"Around there!" I yell in the pause between Fury calls, pointing at a jut in the slope. "Try to leave Soulfall there. Maybe the infidels won't see you!"

His black eyes stare at me, but his face is not expressionless. It is filled with sorrow. "Father."

What a nightmare that he calls me that now.

"*Run!*" I shout as the Fury's call picks back up again.

Aiden does so. I leave him, racing toward the infidels. I see their shouting faces, though I can't hear anything through the cacophony. I come to the edge and leap, but not far enough. I'm sinking fast, and as I fall I look up for my son, hoping to see him.

I don't.

The rock face is before me.

I brace myself.

I'm tumbling down the cliff wall, my vision blurred. I land on something. The world is still spinning. I can't breathe. The Fury is all I can hear. Instinctively, I try to roll away. I think my ankle is broken.

Maybe I shouldn't think that.

Chapter 24

All is purple, and then come the blue flickers, light from the Erebus, and the rocks around me all seem blue, too. I think I got hit in the head pretty hard at some point because I can tell I'm not thinking clearly. My clothes are tatters. I'm a bloody mess.

Q's sword lies beside me. The cave is low, maybe four feet tall. It seems like a nice enough place to hide, or heal . . . or it would be if I could trust that my nightmares wouldn't kill me. Can I stand? I don't think so. My right ankle is swelling badly into Jessica's shoe. The cuts the undead had left on my body sting.

Will the dyitzu find me?

Will a Fury?

Does El Cid know I'm alive?

Did Aiden make it?

Q's sword is dimming. I didn't know they did that. And the flickering blue lights seem darker too. I close my eyes for a second. I'll open them up and see if things get brighter. Not yet. Better give it another minute.

Aiden.

My heart is racing in my chest.

Aiden has turned. He chose his mother. He chose the Archdevil. How terrible he was, his blue eyes black, his skin white as marble. I've lost everything.

I wait for death, or rescue, or something . . . but ain't shit happening. So instead of waiting, I think. Every victory in Hell is a hollow one. I'm aware that, on long enough timelines, even people who don't age are bound to die.

So Aiden left me? So what? In the end, it would have been the same anyway. Even if I'd saved him, he'd end up dead and damned and tortured. Probably, no matter what path I took, he'd eventually end up the demon his mother wanted him to be.

Probably.

Whatever God or the Devil, or whomever the fuck is in charge around here, wants is what will happen . . . I couldn't control that. All I could do was try to give my son every opportunity at happiness I could. All I could do was give him the chance to do whatever he wanted to do, to love whoever he wanted to love, to be whatever he wanted to be.

That was my job.

Don't think I didn't listen when Q was teaching me about virtue. Some things make a horse a good horse. Some things make a person a good person. But let me tell you something. I know there are some qualities which make a man a good father, and though I may have been late to the race, I sure as hell came through at the end.

Maybe.

Or maybe if I really had, Aiden would have wanted to be human.

"Myla. We fucked up. I think he escaped Soulfall. He's a strong boy. He's going to make it. You'll see. Maybe you were right. Maybe I should have just let you be. I guess we'll never know. I guess we might have pulled him too hard in different directions. But he's strong Myla. He's strong. He'll be a great wight. I know he will. He'll kill lots of us . . ."

And with that I find I can no longer lie to myself. The simplicity of my fate strikes me.

I failed.

No infidel would have spared Aiden. That's good, too, because infidels don't cry, and I can't help myself.

I failed.

I'm sorry, Cid. I failed.

Even here, on the edge of the Erebus, I can tell that reality isn't quite as malleable to my mind as it was on Soulfall, but the hellsong is still more or less subjective.

I'm going to have to let him go. This is what he wanted. I wasn't anything like what my parents wanted either, and I turned out okay. Didn't I?

Didn't I?

I didn't.

My missions are over. My quests all failed. I've nothing left to do but die.

"You hear me, Satan?" I shout, my voice echoing oddly in the tight cavern. "You taking requests? Play me something, huh? Just don't make it anything like that Clementine bullshit."

I lean back my head against the stone as Myla's voice starts.

Sometimes, I feel . . . like a motherless child.

Maybe, after the dyitzu kill me, there will be still be some music left for them.

And sometimes, I feel . . . like a motherless child.

I've lost blood. I've lost faith. I've lost my son.

A long ways . . . from home.

Slowly, I lose consciousness too.

A long long ways . . . from home.

Want to be notified when sequels are released? Register as a Citizen at hellsongseries.com

Need to look up a term?
Check out the Gehennic Encyclopedia as a free download on Kindle or view at our website: hellsongseries.com/encyclopedia

Submit your Fan Fiction to contact@ehhknovel.com for possible inclusion into an upcoming magazine.
Details at hellsongseries.com/submissions

Sisyphean
Publishing

Hellsong Series

EVEN HELL HAS KNIGHTS

HELLSONG
BOOK I

Shaun McCoy

"McCoy writes with a passion for action."
—Bonnie Stanard, Author of Master of Westfall Plantation

What is it like to be damned?

Arturus knows.

Born in Hell, Arturus has never had the chance to meet his creator or seek redemption; but that doesn't mean he has no destiny. He lives near the village of Harpsborough, whose people have torn a moment of peace from the unwilling claws of damnation—and damnation wants it back.

Future omens are poor. Infidels roam the wilds, devils are amassing, and the very stones of Hell themselves have begun to break apart. But even while they fight damnation, Arturus and the hunters of Harpsborough find themselves facing off against traitors from amongst their own ranks and a people they thought they'd left far behind.

Look for *Even Hell Has Knights* and continue exploring the Hellsong Universe!

Hellsong Series

Like a character? Want to follow them through the Hellsong universe?

Cris appears in *Even Hell Has Knights* and *March till Death*.

El Cid, Q and Aiden appear in *Knight of Gehenna* and *March till Death*

Shaun McCoy lives in South Carolina. He is an accomplished Pianist, Cage Fighter, Chess Player and Writer. You can check out his fan page at www.facebook.com/shaunomccoy

www.ingramcontent.com/pod-product-compliance
Lightning Source LLC
Chambersburg PA
CBHW021143130626
46554CB00005B/1636